C000006694

SKIN OF DRE

Evelyn Conlon, born in County Monaghan in 1952, is an author of short stories, novels and critical essays; her novels include *Stars in the Daytime* (1989) and *A Glassful of Letters* (1998). Her short stories, which have been widely published internationally, have been collected in three books: *My Head Is Opening* (1987), *Taking Scarlet as a Real Colour* (1993) and *Telling* (2000). She has been awarded Arts Council bursaries, has been writer in residence in several locations and libraries in Ireland, and in Jerusalem, a tutor for creative arts with the Open University, and visiting writer at University of St Thomas, St Paul, USA; she has directed workshops in Ireland, Australia and the US, and is a member of Aosdána.

"Conlon has the rare ability to give her words an almost mythic overtone without ever sounding forced." *The Times*

"She picks some of the threads from the fabric of love and examines them closely, refusing to take refuge in coyness or cliché." *The Irish Times*

"Sharp sinuous writing, full of controlled anger and suddenly opened passion. . . . Committed writing, shot through with original thinking and surreal wit." *The Scotsman*

"Evelyn Conlon excels in exposing the dichotomy between public behaviour and private behaviour." *Fortnight*

"She is one of Ireland's major truly creative writers." *Books Ireland*

Also by Evelyn Conlon

EVELYN CONLON

SKIN OF DREAMS

First published in Britain and Ireland in 2003 by
Brandon / Mount Eagle Publications
Unit 3 Olympia Trading Estate, Coburg Road, London N22 6TZ, England
and Cooleen, Dingle, Co. Kerry, Ireland

10 9 8 7 6 5 4 3 2 1

ISBN 0 86322 306 0

Mount Eagle Publications receives support from
the Arts Council/An Chomhairle Ealaíon.

Cover painting: *View 33 Hotel*, copyright © Simon English 2003
Cover design: Anú Design [www.anu-design.ie]
Typesetting by Red Barn Publishing, Skeagh, Skibbereen
Printed by the Woodprintcraft Group Ltd, Dublin

For Fintan Vallely, Trevor, Warren, Lían, Vivienne

ACKNOWLEDGMENTS

I WISH TO acknowledge the help and support given to me by a number of people while I researched and wrote this book. Firstly, the late Tiernan MacBride, who put me in touch with *Murder at Marlhill, Was Harry Gleeson Innocent?* by Marcus Bourke (Geography Publications, 1993). The fictional elements of Harry Tavey are drawn from the life and death of Harry Gleeson. Tiernan also tirelessly answered my questions about his father's involvement in the case. I am indebted to Marcus Bourke for that book and to the Irish Film Centre for making archive film available to me. Among a number of outstanding works on the subject of capital punishment, three stand out: *The Execution Protocol,* Stephen Trombley (Random House, 1993), *Among the Lowest of the Dead,* David Von Drehle (Times Books, 1995), and *The Hanged Man,* Mike Richards (Scribe Publications, 2002). I would also like to thank Chief Petherbridge for his assistance on a tour of Mountjoy Prison, and the staff of Graterford Prison, Pennsylvania, USA. The inmates of this last institution had, of course, no say in granting me permission to enter their quarters. They surprised me by their courtesy. Members of Amnesty International and the organisers of the Journey of Hope and Reconciliation were unfailingly helpful, as were the participants in the Journey, some of whose stories have been referred to in a fictional capacity.

I am grateful for the award of a residency on the Djerassi Resident Artists Program which allowed me to complete a particularly difficult section of the book. I also acknowledge the assistance of the Arts Council/An Chomhairle Ealaíon, who awarded me a bursary in creative literature and a travel grant which helped enormously.

For accommodation and its trimmings, while researching in New York, I would like to thank Kate O'Callaghan, Patrick Farrelly, Linda

Purney and in particular Janet Noble for the use of her sanctuary when making my first visit to death row. A special thanks to Rita Higgins for easing the burden of car hire.

Cecelia Conlon and Tom MacDonald gave me great hospitality in San Francisco on my way to and from the Djerassi Program. Christopher Fitz-Simon and Sung Joon Whang gave me two great yarns. Andrew Roe bartered GAA tickets for more work typing than he had anticipated.

I would also like to thank my agent, Ania Corless, at David Higham Literary Agency.

For discussion while working, Pat Murphy, Nell McCafferty, Gina Moxley, Patsy Murphy, Mary Holland. A crucially important late reading was undertaken by Pat Murphy, for which I will always be grateful.

When finishing this book, I think of the people who courageously, and against the odds, battle for unpopular causes.

The truth is rarely pure, and never simple.

OSCAR WILDE

CHAPTER 1

MAUD HAD DECIDED what she would say at Dublin Airport if she was asked. It was better to be prepared. She would say that it had all started in her head. That might explain things. Surely they would understand if she talked about her head and not malice aforethought, or premeditation, or other laden words — words were weighted all the time, shot to bits out of recognition with supposition. She didn't know if people were looking at her. She thought they were, but couldn't be certain. There had been news items in the States, continuous ones, as was usual, said so often, in so many places, for such a short time, that one's mind either gave an item monumental status or forgot it altogether. It was hard to tell which way a thing might go. The sun was rising up here over the world, above the clouds, where it always was for hours each day, well hidden from us below by dense, deliberate cumuli.

The two women across from her were looking at their children, stunned into immobility. They rubbed the heads of their babies in wonderment, content enough, not imagining yet what was ahead of them. The young couple on the other side of her did a lot of touching. The man in particular touched the woman's face a lot, did contour feels around her chin. It must be ticklish; it was certainly aggravating to watch. They spoke very little. A voice near by was propounding a strange theory of numerical loss. Take every person in an unhappy relationship, not only were they unfortunate, so too was someone else who was losing out by not being with them. A man was trying to engage another man in a discussion about their boss's personal life. Man number two was having none of it. The more sincere, involved, warmed up, man number one became, the cooler man number two's voice became. These things were consoling, ordinary and consoling. Maud could have been sitting in a café at home, having no airport to go through.

The plane landed with its usual bump, and little excitements gathered force up and down the aisles. The passengers were pleased with themselves, as if they, individually, had done the piloting. Returning emigrants checked their stylishness and congratulated themselves on making one more visit home, never for a moment seeing themselves as the waiting relatives might. Returning workers dwelt on the success of that particular visit to the States and wished, as they visualised their afternoon meeting in the office, that the contrasts of enthusiasm from one side of the Atlantic to the other were not quite so stark.

Maud, surprisingly, and yet not surprisingly at all, named after Maud Gonne, wore black linen trousers, a light grey shirt and a crimson jacket. Doesn't sound like much, but when she finally stood up to leave the plane, anyone with an eye for these sorts of things could see that she had taste and some money. Her blue necklace and earrings caught the colour of her eyes, which twitched occasionally. She could have been nervous or she could have been delighted, as if she had got the better of somebody. It was an Aer Lingus plane; the hostesses smiled at every last one of the disembarking passengers. Maud deliberately jumbled her thoughts on the long trek, almost a mile surely, from the plane door to the luggage roundabout. Were people watching her? She went to the far corner where some smokers had illegally lit up. She sat down and engrossed herself in the pleasure of a cigarette, drawing into her lungs hot dark smoke, watching for her bag, but not too obviously. Were people watching her? Frank, her housemate, and his niece Ailish would be waiting for her. She didn't know why the two of them were coming. She could have got a taxi, or one of them could have come. Surely Frank had more to do than visit an airport as if it was a fulfilling excitement. Perhaps Ailish sensed some drama. That one would be taught a lesson yet. As a first year student, she had come, reluctantly, to live with her Uncle Frank and that woman who shared the house with him. She had been made come by her mother, Frank's sister. She had behaved as if this would be an assault on her freedom, but she was still there, intrigued by something she couldn't understand, seduced by the semi-home that Maud and Frank had made in their jointly owned house. Ailish would have skipped lectures, Frank would have taken the morning off work. They could be waiting a long time.

The truth of the matter is that some day, since that day, she had been going to do what she'd done, or if not that, then something like it. There's no way out of a past, not always the long past. It could be just a brief past of a day, a year maybe, or as in Maud's case, a discovered past, a fact that had been hidden, a fact that threw a new uncomfortable light on almost every single thing of her life, including even her name.

CHAPTER 2

THERE IS NOTHING to be said about Maud's childhood. Her family revelled in the normal oddities in which people luxuriate, having been convinced that these are the very things which make them normal — a bit too much mannerly civility, so it became uppitiness, a slight leaning towards proper pronunciation, or at least a deference in speech patterns to one's betters, which was perceived as snobbery, a more than normal desire for privacy, which was most certainly seen as the thin edge of eccentricity. To think of it now pained Maud like a slap in the jaw. Slap.

Maud and her brother Malachy were twins, not identical obviously, but remarkably alike for a boy and girl. Twinhood gave them confidence. Their mother often said that when they walked away from her in opposite directions, backs turned to her and each other, they always turned around to face her again at exactly the same moment. As they grew older they indulged her by allowing her to repeat this too many times. At secondary school they were considered by the teachers to know too much about the opposite sex; they told each other everything, not being opposite at all. It put a strain sometimes on their dealings with their own. On the school bus, Malachy was too quick to say to boys, "Girls don't think like that" or "That's not what girls think."

Maud was too quick to sigh knowingly, so altering the tempo of fumbling conversations that, with the terrific excuse of ignorance, were just about to triumphantly lurch into sluttishness. Maud and Malachy sat beside each other in the mornings, an action that ravelled the normal run of events, but at least in the evenings they mixed only with their own sex, the day in separate schools having normalised them into behaviour that was more comfortable for their peers. But when they got off the bus together, boys and girls looked at them oddly as the two of them fell into chat even before the driver had pulled off. Androgyny was not an easily understood concept around those parts, at that time. In homes, when children just in from school hurried to mention Maud and Malachy, parents made vague thin hmphing sounds and some said, "Well. . ."

It was Malachy who first got fed up with their lives and longed for a city; it was as if he was older than her, which indeed he was, by a minute. He would have liked to make this part of his life into memory.

"There's nothing to do."

"That's not true. We have the youth club and we get to dances and you have football as well."

"There's no girls."

"Of course, there are girls. They're all over the place."

"None that I like."

"You'll meet someone."

"Where? At some lousy dance somewhere?" In preparation for the city, he was already ashamed of his entertainment.

"I like dances. And I don't know what you're complaining about; you couldn't be found for half an hour when we were leaving the last one."

Malachy scrunched his face up in puzzlement, then said hesitantly, "That's right," as if he had forgotten.

Maud's teasing pleased him. He was happy for a few days. But, irritatingly, his boredom had planted a sense of dissatisfaction that grew in alarming leaps and bounds as the leaving certificate examinations came and passed one by one. Maud hated the thought of parting with her roads, with the seasons that would be camouflaged in a city, with the bedroom that her parents had gradually allowed to become her exclusive corner. It wasn't that she was dependent upon the certainty of her parents; it was just that she liked them and wasn't ready to leave. But they were pleased that she was going into the Civil Service and had already prepared themselves for the departures with what Maud, if she'd known, would have considered disloyal, pre-emptive acceptance. Malachy was going into teacher training; he would always have longer holidays than her.

"I'll do the shopping on Thursdays while you're at work, if you make the tea on Mondays and Tuesdays. I'll cook on Wednesdays, mostly," he said.

Maud said, "We'll have fish and chips or something like

that on Thursdays. You can forget weekends. I'm going home every Friday."

"Not *every* Friday, that's silly. You'll miss the best part of Dublin."

"I'm going home on Fridays."

And so she did, for a while. Maybe her parents shouldn't have spoiled her so when they saw her, changing any and all arrangements to suit the least desire of hers. It made Monday evenings back in Dublin even more bleak than they would have been, what with all the concrete and the flat not warm when she came home. But then there was Malachy, well out and about town by now, and he dragged her into their present and cajoled her into the future. And her work was fine, as long as she realised that work was not meant to be all enjoyment. This may seem neither a radical nor a hard notion to integrate into the shape of a weekly life, but it was a shock to Maud. And a vibrant insult.

Perhaps, too, she had doubts about office work as real work. In an old-fashioned way, she felt that she should be pro- ducing something: milk from cows, vegetables, knitted jumpers, cars, rivets even. Some mornings boredom hung over the office like legionnaires' disease, crescendoing in the after- noon into extraordinary outbursts, half insults swishing about like fish slapping each other in the mouth with back flips. Maud sat opposite a girl who slung her hair back over her shoulder every few minutes. The hair was red and pieces of it staticked out from her crown, making her look as if she had an aura of spiders' webs. She was developing an isolated, unusu- al muscle in her arm from all the slinging. On days that had an abnormal amount of boredom Maud watched the hair a lot. The girl had been reared as a Plymouth Brethren and should not have been so involved with her hair. It was her personal rebellion. At three days of age, her father and aunt had taken her from the nursing home that she shared with her new mother and brought her up to Belfast to have her baptised in the nearest thing to a colony that they could reach. Luckily, she had not caught serious cold, because heaters in cars were not that great then. The gathering of information like this helped to pass the time.

Some of Maud's superiors, including her immediate boss, had an unsavoury smell of ambition coming off them. It was an alien affliction to Maud, and yet she did move up the ladder, partly because her lack of desire to do so was attractive. She was amazed by her first promotion; she couldn't understand what it said about herself. Malachy rubbed his hands, patted her on the back and told her that she was great. His world was already set on one clear line, and his twin sister's promotion could indeed be seen as an integral part of the straight march forward. But Maud was uneasy in the constricted space of an office, was humiliated by the strict adherence to the minute hand on the clock and profoundly irritated by the careless gossip of her co-workers.

Three years passed. Malachy was now a teacher in a primary school, loving almost every minute of it and seeing a headmastership speeding towards him. Men were at a premium in his job, and even if he hadn't been as good as he was, promotion was a certainty, so that small boys would be able to see that men could succeed as the teachers of small children. His optimism grew daily and glowed around him. His blue eyes were full with good thoughts. Love with Valerie, the remedial teacher, seamlessly followed their first date. The only niggle was his sister, but Valerie helped put that in perspective.

"Just because she's your twin doesn't mean that you can live her life."

Exactly. But still.

Maud daily became more fidgety at coffee break; lunchtime was spent walking alone around Stephen's Green. This behaviour was noticed, but her unhappiness was misconstrued as the kind of aloofness associated with the personal grooming of someone who wanted to go further. She got another promotion.

"There'll be no stopping you now," said Malachy.

But Maud came home in the evenings and sat in the hard rocking chair, letting the gloom of the nights gather unchecked into the room. She would rush to put the light on when she heard Malachy coming in. She felt that something was going to happen, something that she wouldn't like.

CHAPTER 3

IT WAS ALMOST a year after the beginning of Malachy's passion for Valerie that the something happened. Maud came out from work one evening and was happy to see Malachy double-parked outside her office, waiting for her. He said, through the open window, that he had just pulled in and was glad to have caught her. She hopped into the passenger seat. She was tickled by enthusiasm.

"Where are we going?" she asked.

The question had no weight to it. But then she caught a sound, a sound of nothing. And then she noticed a darkness about his lips. Or perhaps it was his face that was unusually white. It looked stiff and cold.

"What's wrong?"

She saw his face getting even whiter. Her voice climbed up a few decibels.

"Jesus Christ, what's wrong Malachy, what's wrong?"

Malachy was trying to drag himself through these words. They were like sludge, unknown to him.

"There's been an accident. Our parents."

What an official thing to call them. The formal naming of them held the warning sign up. If she could stop him adding anything further. . . He thought that he would have to say this slowly; after all he was older than her. He put his hand on her arm. It felt heavy.

"Oh, please," she whimpered, and it could have meant, go on, or it could have meant, don't say another word, please just don't say another word, let me go back three minutes, back inside the office, and let you not be waiting here for me with this news.

"They are dead," he said, "both of them. It is better that both of them died together."

She looked at him wildly. Strange beating noises came and went in her ears. She caught his hand and dug her nails into it, then let her fingers fall limp. He lifted both her hands, covered them with his and brought them to touch his face. After a moment they tried to put their arms around each other. It was awkward because of the steering wheel. She noticed that. A driver behind them blew his horn. Malachy said, laying her hands back on her lap, "We will have to go now," as if that was a terrible thing. And he manoeuvred the car out, to start the long journey back to the morgue in their county of origin.

CHAPTER 4

DURING THE WEEKS after the death of P. Joe and Cassie Mannering, time slowed almost to a standstill for Maud. There was an acuteness about each minute. She went back to work, exhausted from all the talking to people, almost looking forward to a desk, office correspondence, an excuse not to dive into answers to platitudinous questions. But there were times when she seemed to go rigid with fear. The feeling might start in her hand or her ribs or her elbow; no matter where, it fanned itself out until her whole body was stiff as a frozen stick. Minutes were like a house of cards: one of them fell, and the game of getting through the next hour collapsed. She felt cold. Everything was new. *This is the first time I have taken an appointment since. . . . This is the first time I have had a tuna sandwich since. . . . This is the first time I have watched the nine o'clock news since.* . . . She heard references to things that had happened a week ago, but they were lost to her, they had never occurred.

The first time she went to the butcher shop, she said, "A pork chop, please." She lifted a dozen free range eggs from the side of the counter and placed them in front of her. The butcher looked at her quizzically as he put the chops beside the eggs. He shivered.

"Someone has just walked over my grave," he said, then laughed nervously.

Maud was terrified. She stammered, "How much is that?"

She hurried from the shop. She felt that she should go back to tell him. Otherwise he would not know what had caused that ripple of cold. He might worry this evening. He might have a nightmare tonight. She did not go back. It was better that some people didn't know what terrible thing had happened to her. But it distressed her to know that her grief was such a living thing that it walked with her and created a disturbance for strangers.

"It will take time," people said, and she wondered what they knew about time.

"Are your parents alive?" she asked.

If only it had been just one of them. She liked people best if they had a mother or father dead. She preferred those who had no parents alive. Both bookends gone.

Malachy stayed home most evenings, although he would have preferred to busy himself away from their flat. They drank too much. Maud opened bottles of wine and marvelled at the greatness of drink, how the first glass vanished pain like a magician might. Towards the end of the third glass the magic wavered, and something like disappointment or a merciless sorrow crowded over them. They needed each other desperately, one to talk, one to listen, to disagree about the sequence of things that had happened, to help each other put order on their pasts, which had become living things and much longer than their actual years. They both knew that this swimming in agony would have to stop, that they could not put their feet up to doom, as if it was a warm fire, but they were reluctant to leave unsaid the things that needed airing and even more loth to take the blind leap into the parentless future. Valerie felt left out, but her workmates advised her to leave them be for a while. It would be better in the long run to let them weep in private. But despite this advice, she worried that one of them would get over the immediate pain quicker than the other; her suspicions about which one it would be changed daily.

The three of them went to the month's mind mass together. As the priest flourished his way through the comforting familiarities, Maud suppressed the memories that were too hard to bear. She dreaded the handshakes with neighbours that were now bound to happen and removed the ring from her right hand so that it did not become sore, as it had at the funeral. But she was surprised to discover how the neighbours' genuine concern made her feel fine, or at least finer. They went to the local pub afterwards, where their parents had had their quiet few drinks every Saturday night, always going home before closing time, an unnatural thing in itself.

Valerie said, "I'll do the driving back to Dublin so that the two of you can have a few drinks with everyone. There's no need for all of us to stay sober."

It was the kindest of offers. On the way to the pub they passed their old house. Maud and Malachy turned together to stare at it. As Valerie drove on, they turned their heads and even looked out the back window. Valerie slowed down.

"Would either of you like to go in?" she asked.

Maud said, "No, not yet. Next week, Saturday, if that's all right with you, both of you."

Valerie had obviously been asked to join them. The house would have to be cleaned up. There was no way out of that. So Saturday it was.

* * *

The house had originally been a cottage, a square cottage, but it had finicky additions, including a half-upstairs, which gave it a body and a face. The roof was crooked in places, and the garden was full. The bushes came right up to the side walls. The assortment of flowers was in almost continuous bloom, decay, bloom. It had always been kept tidy and clean, but not overfussy. As they neared it on that Saturday, Malachy speeded up as if to avoid watching its approach. When Maud got out of the car, she went towards the front door, head bowed, key ready in her hand. She could have sworn there was a washing on the line, flapping, slapping, but that wasn't possible. It was a hard journey from the gate to the door. Malachy stood back and let Maud turn the key. She pushed the door against some letters. Who could possibly have sent letters? Who could possibly not have known? The names on them were too unbearable to be taken seriously.

Maud thought that there were two kinds of mothers, those who could watch their children having injections and those who shiver uncontrollably as they try to lie to their child that it won't hurt. The latter are in serious trouble. Theirs was like that, constantly in love, saying sorry to her children. Malachy heard their mother talking loudly about them when they were teenagers, covering worry. A neighbour had visited once with her young baby. Their mother had put the child on the sofa and said, "Look at you, sitting up there with your great little straight back, and you not six months. You're a genius." She had been like that, giving generous credit where it was not necessarily due.

In the dead quiet of the house, nothing was breathing except the fridge. They had forgotten to switch it off, on the forlorn evening that they had left it. The street outside was empty of teenagers, and because it was a wet windy day, no mothers were taking small children out for a breath. But you could feel them behind the curtains, waiting for a respectable time to pass before they would call to see if anything needed doing. When they had made a cup of tea — Valerie had remembered to bring teabags, milk, scones and butter — real sounds came back into the room. There was an audible shuffle of feet; it could have belonged to the doctors coming down the hospitable corridor to talk to Malachy and Maud on that evening. There had been two of them, one each. Or they could have belonged to the dead and their living children.

"Jesus Christ, the goldfish. We forgot about the goldfish," Maud said, putting her hand over her mouth. All three of them laughed nervously.

"Will we bury them or what?"

Maud remembered them circling the bowl and taking sporadic darts towards each other as if to kiss. It became very important to get them out of the house. Malachy said that he would do it, and when he came back in, the women didn't ask him where nor how. They felt mean for not having offered to go to the garden with him.

"Right then, we'll take a room each," said Malachy, the schoolteacher. Valerie was certainly one of them now. "Stack similar things together. We'll get proper packers in for what we want to keep. Put all the clothes together."

It sounded easy. And despite the occasional strangled cry, it became just a day's work, with breaks for food from the near-by takeaway. Two neighbours did call briefly, but knew to leave them to it, and spread the word to the others.

"We'll be having a drink later, at ten, say. Down in the hotel bar."

And when ten o'clock came, it was all, "What are you having?"

The drinks gave them the courage to stay in the house that night, Maud in her old room, Malachy and Valerie in his.

"I'll start on the boxes in the attic in the morning," Maud said, as if the job would be an ordinary task.

It is presumed, indeed wished, that a person will find at least bones in a dead parent's cupboard. Maud had two parents dead at the same time, not giving one of them a chance to censor, so she knew that she would find some unexplained things in the attic. It was a useful thought. It helped her flick through the paper paraphernalia of a life, two lives. When she found the packet, sternly overwrapped, with layers of paper and sellotape, she knew that this was it. But she had expected maybe love letters from unknown people or a child thing, a birth thing — that was always the big one. This was what she found.

Dear Brigid,

I write this letter with a heavy heart but with some glimmer of consolation, even if it is one that cannot rectify the injustice done. Your brother sent for me last Tuesday evening, and, as I drove over to see him, I was in quite a rage thinking, now he will tell me that he did do it. I tell you this only so you will know that I was not automatically predisposed to believing him. But when I was shown in to see him, I knew by his countenance that I had been wrong to have doubts. He told me that he had been thinking of my possible doubts and that he wanted to reassure me. He had not murdered Moll Graney. He could not, would not, murder anybody, and certainly not his defenseless neighbour whom he had rather pitied, yet admired. But he told me that I was not to carry this with me for the rest of my life, that I had done all that was humanly possibly. He said that there was no point now in going over the details of his defence. He said that he was ready to meet his God and that I could go now. We shook hands. I have never experienced such a handshake.

When I reached the door, he said that if, in time, I felt there was anything I could do, he would appreciate it if I could help to clear his name. It wouldn't matter one whit to him, he said, but it might, to you and children to come. He was serene. He smiled at me. On my way out the governor shuffled more than normal, and told me that he thought that an innocent man was going to be hanged.

I prayed very hard on Wednesday morning, as I am

*sure you did. I will be in touch soon. Rest assured that
I will not let this story rest.*
    Yours sincerely,
    Sean MacBride.

The parcel also included newspaper clippings, further letters from the barrister, a neck tie, a music book, a book on greyhounds and a photograph of a tall man holding a small child.

Maud drew in deep breaths of disbelief. This had to be her mother's uncle. Her mother had had an uncle, one other than Hugh. Her mother had had an uncle, and he had murdered a woman and had been hanged for it. But according to this letter, he had not murdered a woman and had been hanged for it. Her mother had never told them. Her mother's Uncle Hugh had never told them. This man had not just been hanged for something he didn't do; he had been so efficiently airbrushed out of existence he might never have been born.

And the neighbours would have known. All their lives, the neighbours would have known. All their bloody lives, their mother, their mother's uncle, their father, she presumed, had known. Had the neighbours' children known? The people who went to school with them? The people on the school bus? The bus driver with the twinkling eyes and the exciting smell of drink? Their teachers, oh God, their teachers, her first teacher who always told her that she was good at school and would make a teacher herself, the shopkeeper in the shop where they bought sweets? The big fat shopkeeper with the chins rolling down into each other? Had they all known? And had they wondered if she and Malachy knew?

Oh my good God.

Maud sat for a while rereading, unwilling to move from the quiet and must of the room. Although in normal circumstances she would have immediately discussed a matter as important as this, indeed as shattering as this, with Malachy, she put the parcel aside and decided to wait until she had digested the enormity of the discovery before talking to him. It would be best if at least one of them could allow reactions to settle before discussing it. She did not admit that she was a little afraid of how Malachy might react, nor that she had a strong niggling desire not to let Valerie know. Already, having known this thing a mere few minutes, she was doing exactly as her mother had done. The thumping of a person with a secret has effect. Even the act of returning the knowledge to secrecy produces effect. She thought about this as her heart picked up speed, missing some beats and creating a feeling of air in her head. She could hear noises from downstairs, the clanking of pots, pans, crockery, kitchen accessories being arranged together. What would they do with it all?

Rain began to fall, then intensify, becoming the only outside noise. She went downstairs, remarkably steadily, she thought, having picked up a box of photographs which would do to break the ice.

"Remember this," she said, and Malachy and Valerie stood one at each of her shoulders looking at the picture, their physical closeness like a blanket being put over a wet cold body. "This is at Portrush. Our aunt took it, our father's sister, during the war. The telegraph poles were hammered down into the beach so that enemy planes couldn't land. The seals came in, and as the tide was going out, one of them got caught on a pole. This woman, who swam every day, all year round, thought she would save him. She borrowed an umbrella and swam out. Everyone on the shore watched. They were delighted when she managed to poke him off the pole, but no sooner had she turned to swim back towards them than the seal was back again."

Valerie touched Maud on the shoulder. There had been a lot of that this day, touching, holding, hugging. It would have to stop sometime soon. Malachy said, "We have only one aunt on my father's side, and my mother had only one uncle."

"Yeah," said Maud.

They left the house that evening, having decided to make no decision yet about what to do with it.

CHAPTER 5

THE CLOSENESS BETWEEN Malachy and Valerie became urgent. It physically filled evenings and nights, and the thought of it hung around daytimes. It was becoming an edifice. A marriage was being rehearsed as a means of structuring thoughts. They didn't decide to move in together. Or if they did, they certainly didn't tell Maud. Valerie merely moved out from her old flat into a bigger one, and Malachy stayed over one night a week, two nights, eventually seven. He did try to bring the subject up with Maud. He wanted to check that she would be all right. She seemed distracted and strangely happy to see him move the last of his shirts out. He would have been hurt if the pleasures attached to moving in with Valerie had not been so great. It wasn't that Maud wouldn't miss him, it was just that her thoughts were elsewhere. She, too, was preparing, but her engagement was with the past. She felt that she had no choice. She wondered sometimes if she could ignore the overwhelming curiosity that was with her all day and that informed her sleep, but finally it seemed wiser to tackle it.

She became diverted at times by her immediate past, by grief. That past was a time when she could still have picked up a telephone anywhere and spoken to her mother, taken for granted the sound of her voice, exchanged weather reports, each of them having different things to say, titbits of gossip about people her mother only knew by repute and people that she, Maud, should definitely remember. *Of course, him*! This time would never be again.

She got angry, not just at death, but at secrecy. How had her parents kept it up? The hypocrisy of it! How could she believe anything else they had ever said? What type of people kept such secrets? Any wonder they had gone home early from the pub on Saturdays. Was it a fear that one more drink might push one of them into inappropriate conversational intimacy with a neighbour? Or was there a tacit understanding that the last drinking moments needed to be left to the neighbours alone, so that one of them would chant a ritual "Terrible thing altogether".

Had that been their hope? The anger became a pointless thing, an aggravating, unsatisfactory emotion that explained nothing. Maud bought a hardback notebook and started making plans. She would get to know a man who was her uncle. From scratch. Granduncle, uncle, same thing.

* * *

The National Library hummed with the sound of people working out their ideas.

"A hanging. In the forties. Let me see, the best place would be. . ."

It was a tremendous thing to know that the hanging involved herself. Tremendous in the sense of colossal rather than wonderful. The newspaper reports were steady and unemotional. The tale unfolded, letting people know that there was a beginning, a middle, and that there would be an end. There were facts and no diversions. Maud would have to piece those together as one would learn, say, a new religion.

The facts were as follows: Rita McGrane, born 1902 to an unmarried mother, reared in an orphanage in Clonmel, became Moll Graney, a woman who once had one child, then two children. She procured food for them by having intercourse with their fathers and others, thus putting herself in the way of having more children, thus needing more food and money for clothes. She loved her children more wisely than she lived her life. Perhaps wisdom cannot play any role in the circumstances of a life hemmed in by poverty and its restraints. We do not know if non-maternal love or even pleasure were ever known to her. She was murdered between Wednesday the twentieth November 1940 and Thursday the twenty-first. She had been shot in the head with a shotgun. Her face and head had been brutally blown into death. The state pathologist vomited after seeing her. Harry Tavey, her nearest neighbour, was charged with her murder at the local court. The case was sent to Dublin and tried before a judge and twelve city men, who found him guilty. His appeal failed. He was hanged in Mountjoy jail on a Wednesday morning, five months after the crime had been committed.

These were the facts that Maud now knew. This was the happening that had ended the life of Moll Graney and wiped Maud's granduncle from the breathing earth and from memory itself. These were the facts that caused the letter to her grandmother which she had found in her mother's attic.

Maud could get up in the morning, get ready and go to work. She could do her job efficiently, be appreciated for it, depended upon, eat light lunches, go for walks. She could have a night in every week, have a long bath, pluck her eyebrows, cut her toenails and manicure her hands, as a visiting beautician to her secondary school had once advised. Maud did do these things, diligently, sometimes even with a sense of satisfaction and pleasure. She went to the pictures regularly, talked normal talk, went for drinks with Malachy, or Malachy and Valerie, cured occasional headaches and pampered herself with hot water bottles when demanded. But the facts would never go away.

She bought books about the psychology of murder, began searches for the flesh and feeling of these facts, read a book of letters to and from death row. Malachy tossed it from the couch before he sat down. He was visiting to discuss their parents' house, what the next move should be, or should they leave it another while, allow it to grow into a monument?

"A little light reading I see," he said, a tinkle of annoyance sounding in his voice.

"Yes, it's interesting," Maud said. "They've started using chain gangs again in Alabama. You can see them shackled to each other from the highways, swinging their mattocks, clearing brush. And when some people complained about these men being so near the open road, they were told it was okay, they're not dangerous criminals. Well, if they're not dangerous criminals, why have their legs langled?"

"Gosh," Malachy said, absentmindedly. "Where did you read that?"

"In a magazine."

"What magazine?"

"Oh, an Amnesty International thing, I think."

"Really."

He went back to Valerie's flat and said that his sister was becoming strange.

"She was never the most normal," Valerie said, and Malachy resented that. And Valerie knew that he didn't like it, but she was saturated with love, making her sly. She was afraid that the love might go away.

* * *

Maud bought a car. This took up a lot of time. People advised her so much she became muddled. She thought that one would just go to the garage and point to a car and say, "I like that one" or "That colour is nice." But there was horsepower, horsepower to do with tax, insurance, power steering, four door or two door, diesel or petrol. Maud wanted a black car with a radio. Malachy told her that it was a very good idea. Secretly he thought that it was about time. His sister had accrued so few possessions it was almost peculiar. Maud's reason for buying the car was that it would be easier to drive up and down to Tipperary than to depend upon buses. Indeed, it was essential to have a car, because she didn't know where she would be going. She presumed that she wouldn't be able to walk into the local pub and ask about the murder and the hanging. The pub might belong to a state witness, or one of Moll Graney's children. Unlikely. Still. Or a guard's son who was touchy. Or the descendants of a neighbour who changed after the trial, became uneasy.

Driving lessons were terrifying at first. They took her mind over, more even than a diet would. Her neck got sore, she broke out in sweats, her eyes were stiff. She would get the hang of the clutch, then she would lose it on the next gear change, like someone learning to walk again after an accident.

"Have you ever used a sewing machine?" the instructor asked, the exasperation in his voice as thinly veiled as young ice. But she got there. She failed the test the first time, and everyone told her about statistics, as if it had nothing to do with the fact that she had overtaken a car at the lights, crossing a continuous white line. She got her licence the second time.

It was unfortunate that on her first journey to New Inn it snowed. The road seemed narrow, and the trees were ominous in their heaviness. The wheels didn't appear to belong to the car, and her mind sometimes went blank with fear. But after fifty miles she was stroppy enough to think that it could have been worse, it could have been fog, or that thing the news-readers always called black ice. Black ice sounded bad, like ships sheltering off Land's End in a gale force ten. Black ice could get you. There was a purr coming now from the car, and she could imagine the muffled crackle of the tyres on the snow. She would have liked to open the window, to hear it clearer, but she was afraid to take her right hand off the wheel. She would never recognise this road again; it would be different without white trees. She pulled into a side road to check the map. The heater was a homely comfort in the loneliness, but was there something about people suffocating in parked cars with heaters running, or would that take hours? Yes, she was near. She would now look for a B&B; she didn't want to get too close until morning.

A hotel would have been a better idea. Hotel receptionists rarely ask questions, and if they do, they do it by rote and either do not hear the answer or forget it immediately. B&B women ask fiddly things in such a way that it is rude not to reply. And they remember everything.

"Visiting friends?"

"Yes."

"Near here?"

"Yes."

"There are not many places near here."

"Oh."

"An old school friend?"

"Yes, yes."

"What school would that be?"

"Boarding school, away."

"Would you like a cup of tea?"

Maud would have loved one, but had no intentions of accepting, because she would then be a sitting target for more questions. This was truly a stupid thing to be doing, scary, too. What does a wild goose chase mean? Who is chasing the goose, and are wild geese that elusive? Oh, there were lots of things she could think. It really was an achievement to have driven this far. Her first long journey, and it had been over snow. Motorists are advised not to travel unless their journey is absolutely necessary. Was hers?

Yes, it was. Maud knew that she could have ignored the letter. It certainly was an option. It must be. And she also knew that her search probably had to do with loss. But the stubbornness that had set into her was also helpful. It gave her things to think about. Unreasonable stubbornness moved life on. The B&B woman thought that such short answers were just downright bad manners. See if she cared. God knows sometimes it was a trial opening the doors of your house to every stray off the road. A home was supposed to be a place with locked front doors, and they rarely appreciated the sacrifices you were making. Some of them were OK, men mostly, they answered questions at least, maybe they thought them unimportant, maybe they thought her unimportant, the bloody cheek of them. She was whisking herself into a right bad temper. There were some questions you wouldn't ask them though. Men were too busy to be bothered with her little questions, needles of questions.

"Your bedroom is this way."

See if she cared if that strange woman had a cup of tea or not, a cup of tea wasn't too much to offer. At least she had said that the room was nice. There were some manners buried in her somewhere. What was a woman doing out driving at this hour of the night anyway? No rings either.

Maud snuggled into her bed. Leaving home on a mission could be a dangerous thing. Was this a mission? But the State should not be able to hang someone for something he didn't do. If they had even given him the choice of exile, like old times. To be a troubled, red-eyed man looking over vast stretches of foreign land, but alive. The State. That was a dangerous word. Good God, using that word was like something an anarchist would be doing. Was it possible that she was becoming an anarchist? What a frightening thought. Could something make a person into an anarchist overnight? Maud had a surprisingly comfortable night.

The first man that Maud met spilled the story out of him as if it was a streel of words that had been burning his insides. She had tracked him down from the newspaper report, then the electoral register, although she wasn't sure if it was him. It was him all right. The man who came to the door was in his late seventies. His white hair was yellow in spots.

"I don't know how to put this," Maud said.

"Well, the world loves a tryer," the man said. He was twinkling at her.

"I wonder if you are the Brian Mathews who gave evidence at a trial in the nineteen forties." The twinkle went off.

"That'll be Tavey." He became solemn. "Come in," he said, and shuffled before her into his kitchen.

"Yes, that's me. Come on in. Sit down, take the weight off your feet." He pointed to an armchair. "Well, well, how did you find me? And who are you?"

"I'm his grandniece. I didn't know about him when I was growing up."

"Weren't you lucky."

And maybe he is right, Maud thought.

"Would you like anything, a drink, a cup of tea?"

"No, thanks."

He had level eyes.

"Do you dance?"

Maud was startled. She wondered if he was mad. Was he going to ask her to waltz.

"No," she answered sharply. He surely couldn't believe that she could be that easily side-tracked.

"I see. It's just that Harry was a great dancer. He could always get a lift in his feet. A good solid dancer, not that he got much chance. We always wanted him for playing. The women found it hard to forgive us. Couldn't we have got some other fiddler and left him free? He played some tunes better than others, but he could make a right fist of most. He was mad about his greyhounds, too, out at the crack of dawn exercising them in all weathers. What with one thing and the other, he was always busy. He didn't hang around much with the fellas, not being originally from here. He went home every now and again. I saw him buying sweets to take to children. No, it wouldn't have been you, too young. Your mother maybe, or her cousins."

And their children? She wondered if they had known. She would leave them until after Malachy. Maybe they did; maybe that's why they were all such nervous people.

"He was a good farmer. Work done when it should be, sometimes even ahead of himself. But we didn't mind. We put it down to him being a stranger. He worked his aunt's farm, but you know that."

He had forgotten that she knew nothing of the man. So that aunt would have been her great grandaunt. She was gone from the history, too.

"There was another cousin, I think, a younger fella. They say that he was beaten up when the questioning was going on. His horse was tied up outside the barracks all day. He came out of the station in a shocking state. They say he tried to do something about it later. Someone should have told him it was a dangerous thing to go accusing guards of lawbreaking. I don't believe it ever came to anything."

Brian Mathews paused, but only briefly. He had taken a run at his story and wasn't going to be stopped. The relief had overcome him.

"Harry was a fine-looking man, a fine-looking man, and he would have fallen in for that big farm, too. It was good land as well. And well kept. The hedges were always in order. You never saw their cattle on the long acre."

Maud was silenced, not just by the speed of the man's talk but by the pictures, the landslide of pictures of her kin. She would have to tell Malachy soon; this secret could burst her.

"It was a terrible thing about Moll, foxy Moll we used to call her. But some of them tried to burn her out before. People didn't like the way she was living. All those different fathers. Not in a place like this. She was even read from the altar. No one ever said that it was Harry who tried to burn her out; they knew it wasn't him. But even if that kind of living was too much for around here, no one wanted her dead. No one wished that on her. Well, I suppose someone did, but not the most of us. We're not that kind of people."

Maud wondered would it be a better or a worse thing for her to belong to someone murdered. She thought that she would have preferred to be related to Moll. *I wonder what would Malachy think?* Sometimes she despised the part of her that needed her twin, that needed to halve the knowing of things with him. What would she do if he died first? She wouldn't know where he was, if he was thinking of her. Even after the blunting of grief she would clock in the rest of her life half-heartedly.

"I don't think any of us ever really thought that Harry did it, not even at the time, but it all happened so quickly. The hearing was gone from here up to Dublin so quickly, before any of us had time to catch our breaths. And there were rumours, rumours neatly spread, so that we didn't know what was what and only wanted to have nothing to do with it and have it all over. And someone wanted us to think it was Harry, two people, or more even, they say now. All in all, it suited well. He wasn't from around here so it was easier. But I don't think we thought it would go that far. I don't think that we thought the whole thing would be finished in such jig time. When we realised how far gone and serious things were, after the Dublin verdict, we tried to muster ourselves. We even got a meeting with the minister, but it was too late then. If only we'd thought of it sooner, instead of gabbling away surmising."

He shook his head, seeing a man come to middle life, maybe even a family, and no terrible heavy spot hanging over this townland. Maud shivered, imagining a man hanged without cause, and wondered if hanging would be easier if you knew you were innocent. Silly, what difference would it make? Remorse would probably grow into you if you were guilty. Self-pity would be more likely, if you were innocent. Anger would be there, too, of course, but the fear would surely be the same.

"Did no one stand up for him?" she asked.

"Privately, behind closed doors, a few. Some families around here still just nod to each other, and half the younger ones don't know why. It made us tight. The odd night it was rehashed in the pub, some of us would whisper away to each other, but what good did it do, so we stopped after a few years.

A lot of the old ones are dead, the ones who doubted most. Tim Molloy is gone, he was the most certain. He tried to talk to the guards, but they wouldn't listen, or had their own reasons for not believing him. And what's one man against the whole crowd who wanted to believe it was an outsider who had done it? There's no other excuse."

It was getting dark, a huffy grey dark that tried to make up its mind whether to snow or beat up a cruel windy drizzle.

"Will it snow again?" Maud asked. This man would know the signs.

"Too cold, lassie, I think, too cold. It'll freeze though, later on when the light goes, if light is what you'd call that damp out there. Have you far to go?"

"I think I'll go back to Dublin."

"Ah, Dublin. I believe the traffic is terrible. I used to go to the odd match. I was at the court, you know. I might feel better if I'd stayed away."

Maud took a deep breath and plunged into her last question.

"Do you have any thoughts about who might have done it?"

After all, this man or men would have gone on to live.

"None. None."

Maud didn't believe him.

"And did they go on to have children?"

The silence twisted into an accusation, yet she took her leave with less awkwardness than might have been expected. She wrapped up the last few minutes with small talk. He would have liked her to stay longer, but knew that he had no right.

"Goodbye, I hope I'll see you again. Have a safe journey."

Maud decided not to go back to Dublin yet. There were more people she needed to see, and she could do it all tomorrow. Better to have all this done before talking about it. She went back to the same bed and breakfast. Better the divil you know. The B&B woman was astounded. *What the hell is this strange woman at? Still wandering about. Friend my eye! The cheek of her really, to come back here.*

"If I'd known you were coming back, I wouldn't have had to change the sheets," she said.

"Oh, I couldn't find my friend's place. I'm going to have another look tomorrow."

A likely story. Still, she had at least made an excuse. Friend my arse. The landlady was silently descending into inappropriate language. *A man, probably, that's what it was. And not above board, you could bet on that.*

CHAPTER 6

MAUD HAD A sense of humour. She wasn't best known for it, but it was there, lurking unminded in the space between what she thought and what she said. It took a perceptive person to jolt it into the open, where it manifested itself more as a grinning, secretive irony than downright sidesplitting loud public laughter. Left too much to her own devices, as now, her humour got buried by worry. She worried about the accumulation of the facts of her uncle, worried that she wasn't doing enough about getting more of them, worried about being sidetracked, worried about whether she should try to find out who did murder Moll Graney. But she decided that that job had belonged, and would belong again, to the guards. What could she do if she found out? What good would it do her? She was now immersed in the literature of present day executions, up to her neck in hanging, so to speak. America mostly, because they killed prisoners there in the same language in which her granduncle had died. Because of the secrecy of her delvings, there was no one to shake her out of her worry. She would have to do it herself. She began to look for reliefs. Could it be possible that the reasons she had been promoted to a higher grade and moved to the Department of Justice were the greatest laugh out? Was there someone in the department who knew all about her past and thought that it would be great crack altogether to entangle her irrevocably in the very web that did nothing about letting an innocent man go back to his fields, his greyhounds and his music? She prepared for a works party.

Dress shops were a chore. She picked garments off hangers depending on their colour, the lowness of the neckline. One eighth of an inch too deep, that would disappear down into the crack of her bosom, leaving her uncomfortable on the night, but a half an inch too high would make her look nervous or dowdy. The fashion expert in her newspaper said that some women should never wear sleeveless dresses, but what would he know? And what business was it of his anyway? Shop assistants looked around the dressing rooms, making sure that she didn't take more than three articles of clothing in with her. They didn't help her to get different sizes. Each time she had to put her clothes back on again and go forage for herself. Other women had helpers with them, helpers who negotiated the turning in of the wrong size and the re-collection of the allowed number of things, some of them ones that the buyer would never have dreamt of but might, just might, like. In the dressing room she didn't hide her body. It wasn't a perfect shape by any manner of means, but she was happy enough seeing the whole of herself in the long mirror. She would have to get a size up in knickers because tight pants made the bulge on her legs more noticeable. A bigger size would be fooling herself, but no one was nightly watching the unparcelling of her flesh, so she could afford to be lenient, and a dress costing a few extra pounds would hang off her hips and flow the increased fat into a contour. A new slip. There was nothing like silk next to a woman's body.

The hairdresser asked her how she would like her hair cut. *In complete silence*, she thought, but would never have said.

The hairdresser parked her body behind her neck, snipped contentedly, and told Maud all about her holidays. Maud wondered if hairdressers' holidays were always more action packed than anyone else's, or whether they were simply better liars.

"I'd like a bit of a change. Nothing too drastic, but a change."

"Oh, good. I'm new here, this is my first week. In my last job they'd scream, 'What are you *doing*?' if I moved their partings a hair's breadth."

The shoe shop was easier.

At the party she was, as usual, not particularly noticeable. Gradually, she was made cheerful by the fair to middling wine that tasted better the more she drank. There was a substance to the taste, unlike gin and tonic which had no bite. People talked wholeheartedly about what was happening in the country, as if their personal opinions could have made it happen differently. They weren't hard on themselves. Unlike Maud, who occasionally forgot that she was at a party and wondered how men could annihilate a prisoner and then go home for their tea. Or would they have a load of drink before facing home? After an execution would they have hours to hang about filling in forms before they could get to the pub? How soon afterwards would they have a shower, wash their clothes? Would they think about the man that night, or would it be a week later before a very clear picture of the fright in his face would flash before their eyes? Did they have more drink then? Did their jobs give them beer bellies? They wouldn't think very consistently of healthy living. And what about the doctor? Did it worry him that he was breaking his oath, or did he wriggle his conscience to fit into the idea that it was better for him to see it done as quickly and painlessly as possible? And what about the priest? Did he try to pray harder?

"Another glass, Maud?"

"Yes, yes."

The talk grew and slid into comfortable familiarity, the sort that terrifies outsiders. Maud had seen a play called *The Hour that We Knew Nothing of Each Other*. There could be one called *The Hour that We Knew Nothing of It*. The big secret.

"Where are you going on your holidays?"

Holidays, holidays, was there no end to them? Those who are not happy have to pretend hard at parties. A married person who regrets the state but knows that it would take too much nerve to change it. A single person who spends too many evenings being lonely, who always has time, at the drop of a hat, to visit sick relatives in hospital, and who sometimes plays patience addictively.

"God, Maud's a bundle of laughs tonight."

Maud overhead the remark but wasn't particularly annoyed by it. She allowed that the speaker had a point, and she quickened her efforts at being sociable. In the end she got drunk and laughed with the best of them. When her name was called for her taxi, no one noticed her leaving.

In the morning she thought that she had talked too much. What was the point in baring one's ideas like that to people who wouldn't remember a thing about them, or would mix them up with someone else's opinions? But some of the jokes had been good, if only she could remember them. And yet it didn't matter. The act of laughing out loud so much had turned her view around a corner. More action was needed.

CHAPTER 7

MAUD SAT IN the restaurant waiting for Malachy. She held her ankles tight together as if they were wires wrapped around each other. She smoked hurriedly, listening anxiously for the recognisable fall of his feet as he would come to her table. She had her back to the door, not watching it. She preferred to hear him behind her, feel the brush of his hand on her shoulder, like a moth's wing in a dream, rather than to work herself into a temper thinking about his lateness. She wanted to be unhindered, to be ready to catch his attention. Before sitting down she hadn't known that she would not really mind the wait, that it would become a shelter in which to order her thoughts. It would have been lovely to have had simple things to think about in the waiting time: the memory of the noise of scraping buckets from the farm next door, cows lowing away, sounding like trombones tuning up, money for the pictures on Saturdays, their first Tayto Crisps, their first Flashbars, newly arrived to the shop, Malachy's scabby knee at their confirmation, the stitches on the side of her nose for sympathy, lists of things to buy for school at the end of summer, busyness in the jaws of Christmas, the gurgling change in their parents' voices when Lent was over. She really was a little afraid that Malachy might blame her.

A woman was left by her husband in their townland. She had five children. She lost her temper one day and walloped a few of them over the legs. She then marched them down to the priest's house, rang the doorbell, and when he came shuffling to it she still didn't lose her nerve. When he clanked the door open she said, not batting an eyelid, "You take them. You're always yapping on about the sanctity of marriage and the importance of rearing children, so here you are, they're yours."

The priest was as nice as ninepence, took them in for tea and biscuits and called the doctor. The mother spent the rest of her life trying to make it up to her children for that day. Maud wondered if Malachy knew that story or had their mother told them different things?

By the time Malachy came she had dealt with the threads and jagged edges of her day, a process that, when magnified, put the whole of her life, not just the twenty-four hours, into a manageable sort of installation. She knew how she would tell him. But he crept up behind her and took her by total surprise.

"That would never do," he said cheerfully. "The Cubans were ready for the Americans."

Maud wasn't ready for Malachy. After all, he really did think that it was better that their parents had died together.

"The dinner is on me, I've got a salary raise."

"I think the way you say it is, 'I've got a rise in salary.' Did you know that salary comes from salt? When people were paid in salt, I suppose."

"God, you're a mine of information."

She didn't tell him. *Damn.*

CHAPTER 8

MAUD THOUGHT THAT she would like to know more about the lawyer. He had believed in the innocence of Harry. He knew what innocence was.

The lawyer was used to badness. Preserving the trappings of childhood was not a luxury that had been applied to him. He had carried the amputated limbs, arms and legs, to the dump in his mother's field hospital, set up in a casino in France, during the First World War. He was at it for a fortnight, at least, before she found out.

"I told you he could run messages, not that," she sighed brokenheartedly. But it was too late. He knew now. His mother was Maud Gonne. Maud Mannering's mother had named her thus. Was it foolhardy or was it a comfortable wrapping for her secret?

In boarding school in Paris, the Jesuits had told him, in as kindly a way as possible, that his father had been executed. They included his father in the prayers for all the dead fathers and explained that, although England was an ally of France, this boy's country had a separate legitimate fight with England. It was an important statement and taught him something about the consolation of truth. The priests were kind to him. That helped more than a little. Later he became a soldier for his country, not a legitimate one, of course, because that cannot be during the volcanic stages of reaching for statehood.

If childhood is worth remembering, his memory was worth a fortune. It stood up straight, vivid and stiff, for the whole of his life. He would always have a desire to explain himself. Others might do what they did and excuse themselves to no one; he would give reasons. In those days, evening conversation was planned, and the why, not just the what, was important to him. He was reared on poetry and politics, a good mix, he thought. During his soldierly jail sentence in Mountjoy he was asleep in a cell one night with Rory O'Connor. The soldiers woke him up; the governor came in. They were to get ready. But then he was told to stay in the cell. Rory O'Connor wanted to give him his gold coins. But Sean said that he would need them himself, and he sewed them into Rory's belt. The Seychelles had been offered to the new government to house the unrelenting republicans. He could use his gold coins there. The four men, Rory and three others, took books, blankets and a chess set with them for their journey. Next morning, on his way into mass, the soldiers looked at Sean and looked away. He noticed that they had mud on their boots. The priest asked him if he had not heard the shots that morning.

After mass a row broke out between himself and the priest, who wanted him to sign a document recognising the government. The priest was highly distressed because the men had been executed on the Feast of the Assumption and canon law expressly forbids execution on a feast day. As if the day mattered more than the deed. The argument continued as they walked down the stairs and out the door. No conclusion was reached. The prisoner walked back to the door, knocked and was given re-entry. "Shock," he said afterwards. He was so shocked he hadn't realised that he had been outside the gates. He hadn't run. The warders were jittery with shock, too.

Later, forty prisoners almost achieved freedom, but they were found out. All Republican prisoners were on hunger strike. After five days they were cold. The governor ordered that the heat be turned on. There was something wrong with the burner.

"Well, fix it."

The bagloads of clay, the working washroom for the tunnellers, all found. While being removed to Kilmainham Jail, he and a mate saw a chance and made good their escape this time. Two soldiers of the new state met them.

"Hit us, hit us," they whispered urgently, and lay down like good soccer players. As they tiptoed up Cabra they met a gas-lamplighter.

"Talk about the dance."

"How do we know there was one?"

"I said, talk about the dance."

Earlier, when running up a quiet back lane, they had taken off their shoes. Sean's mate had not managed to get his back on and was holding them in his hand, extended in front of himself, for all the world like a man carrying a tray.

"The music was good. Wasn't the music good?"

They reached a safe house. The man of the house opened the bedroom window in reply to the urgent knocking. Sean said who he was.

"Well, if you are, you'll be able to speak French. Where are you coming from?"

"*On vient de prendre le large il n'y a pas si longtemps que ça.*"

"*Ah! C'est pour ça qu'on a entendu des gens qui couraient partout et des coups de fusil.*"

Three minutes chat, the man of the safe house glad to have the opportunity to brush up his grammar. And still a pair of shoes were being held at arm's length.

"Who is it?" a woman's voice called.

"Escapees."

"Will you for Christ's sake let them in and stop nattering."

The woman of the house put two plates of chicken and lard on the table. Their hunger strike was over. They were out a long time. Yes, he knew life. But this prisoner, his client, Harry Tavey, did not. And he had done nothing. He had no reserves, no mates, no training, no understanding that the State could, and indeed would, kill him in the wrong. He knew nothing of escape. He waited for the right thing to be done.

CHAPTER 9

MAUD STRUGGLED WITH the day. There was the price to pay for last night's fun. A sense of sadness dribbled over the morning, and moments of panic had to be controlled. Of course, they had drunk too much. The people troubled only by care of themselves had approached alcohol with interest. She had attacked it as a means to oblivion. Foolish really, because it never lasted, and the price of coming back into the clear was ferocious. But she was being too hard on herself. Once she admitted that the story had got into her brain, like a paralysis, it was easier to wade up to the daylight, to emerge from the drag of her thoughts. Maybe she should buy a dog, or a cat, get a name ready for it. Or grow plants. They could thrive away while she was at the office, grow secretly while she was out. She tried to pamper her heart in order to give her head a break. Cats, dogs, plants, living things. She had liked cows a lot when young. Goldfish were too tiny to hug, but they were colourful. There would be a feel of them breathing in her room.

She went to bed early that night and took the books from the bedside locker. *The Execution Protocol* and *Among the Lowest of the Dead.* She became a tourist in the nether world between men waiting to die and men waiting to kill them. The men waiting to die do so with individual traits, wrung into them by their different lives, their different murders. A man who murdered by mistake may be angrier than another, but maybe not. A man who has had love or letters may have traces of serenity. A man with humour may shrug a little and place his hands on his hips when he talks. What does an innocent man do? What had Harry done? A man may develop a one on one with God. One man rings his lawyer when they read out the black edged pronouncement; they'd spelt his name wrong. Could that help his appeal? How long can a stay last? Another rings a penfriend called Mary and jokes about his wife. Mary collapses into tears at the thought of the news he has just received. He shouts, "What the fuck are you crying about? It's me who has just got the letter, not you."

And the women, what do the women do?

But the men waiting to kill them show less individualism. They're involved with engineering and are encouraged to take a limb apiece, look after it, so that they don't feel as if they've had a part in the demise of a whole person, just a limb apiece. A designer of electric chairs told his interviewer, "Capital punishment, not capital torture is my motto; do the job right and fast. No bungling. My wife's a diabetic, she has to watch her sugar, she drinks lots of Diet Coke, a lot of Diet Coke. I never knew much about diabetes before this."

Because Maud's mother was dead, Maud had less behind her than she ever knew she had when it was there. But because of that death she now also had her granduncle, who seemed more alive, more necessary, because she had never known him, and because of the manner of his death. If her mother had still been alive, Maud would have let her deal with it. But then, of course, she wouldn't know these things if her mother was still alive. The package would still be sitting protected in the attic. As it was, she now had the unbearable but exhilarating freedom to do the necessary, whatever the necessary might turn out to be. A scalding in history. She would pick her man, a live man on death row, communicate with him and see what happened. She had to move things one step further.

She wrote to Life Lines and said she was interested in communicating with such a man. She had to start and restart the letter several times, in an effort not to make it appear as if she was thirteen, looking for a suitable pen pal, one who would share her interests and might turn out to have exotic foreignness. The organisation wrote back, asking her personal, fidgety questions, necessary, they said, because a person needed to have the right motive, be stable and prepared for the projected outcome. Cruel things might happen as well as the death itself. Why, one old couple had communicated with a prisoner for years. They were not informed of the actual day and date, and had their last letter to him returned, boldly marked "Deceased" on the outside of the envelope. Would she be able to deal with cruelties like that? Maud lied where necessary and was deemed suitable.

She got her man and began her letters. He was thirty-four. He had burgled a house when he was seventeen, when he was mortal, sullen and stroppy. The man of the house had attacked him, as Xavier could now see would be what you would do. Xavier had panicked, fought back, and the man got killed. "No, let me rephrase that. I killed him."

If it was any consolation, the dead man's wife didn't want him electrocuted. She went on tours, they called them the Journey of Hope. Once a year, she and other relatives of murdered people travelled to a selected state and asked listeners not to believe in capital punishment. They talked in schools, libraries, churches. They went to states that were cranking up their execution numbers. They seemed to move people away from the "fry them" mentality. They could see spots of light making their audience uneasy, tugging them out from behind the retribution industry.

The wife of the man he murdered said, "Don't get me wrong. I might kill him myself if I got my hands on him, but that is not the same thing. The State is taking my feelings and constructing their own evil with them. And my feelings are not evil. They cannot do this with my feelings."

Things were not looking too good for Xavier. There was an election soon. The governor was wavering. People were baying on his walkabouts, knocking on his door; there were votes in it. Things were not looking good.

In all truth, Maud was glad that her man wasn't a serial killer. She thought about this at her desk in the civil service, as if it was relief similar to that which she could get when it wasn't a wet morning and traffic was moving smoothly into the centre of the city. It is a fortunate thing that thoughts don't have lights on them. The noises of the office acted as a calming spray the morning that the first letter arrived. There is a safe place where people agree on their beliefs, support each other in what should not be touched, what lines are the edges of hopscotch. Maud had just dived out of that place into the unknown. Alone. At least so far, alone. But there would be people like her, and she would find them. But they would not be people like any that she had met before. She might be unsure among them. Old friends would be horrified and would have stand-offs about who had dropped her fastest and first, about who wasn't going to have anything to do with that kind of thing. What would Malachy think? Not yet, not yet. She had to be surer, more able to resist his outrage. She would pick her time, maybe during the summer, when the long evenings would give him more time to simmer, or on a night before he went away on holidays. If he was going with Valerie to France, say, or Italy, surely they would have more to do there than think about her, her and the secret, the secret that so far she was protecting every bit as fiercely as her mother had done, as if it was a family heirloom.

But summer was far away. Maud's time was now packed with new knowledge, stretching days into longer hours than they had ever had before. That would make summer very far away.

CHAPTER 10

MAUD SLEPT ALL the way across the Atlantic. This should not have been the case. When the captain said seven and a half hours, she was bitterly disappointed. People said that it took five. Apparently Valerie's old neighbour from childhood had recited six rosaries on her first journey over. She must have been slow at praying or staunch in her adherence to trimmings. But tiredness did eventually come over Maud. The efforts of deception these last three weeks had exhausted her. Everyone thought she was going on a holiday to New York, and wasn't that great? Malachy had bent each and every way to form excitement around her journey. Valerie had surpassed herself in trying to fit in, in trying to pretend that she could understand the strangeness of her fiancé's sister. Twin sister. Fiancé without the ring, but it was coming; it was in the atmosphere, it was almost there.

At Valerie's insistence, Maud and she went shopping, in preparation for the holiday. It made a change from getting in and out of clothes alone in dressing rooms, going half dressed to racks. Maud rather liked it. They surmised about temperatures in New York. They gathered warnings about the dangers of the city and swapped them like priceless wonders. A place where you kept your keys in your pocket until you were right bang smack up against the door. But you had your hand on them, and the right one between your thumb and first finger, so you could get the door opened quickly. Imagine a place so dangerous. You should walk quickly, smartly, with purpose, as though you knew where you were going. That would be interesting, striding down streets where you would meet no one you knew.

"Would you not stay with my cousin?" Valerie said.

"No. It wouldn't be like a real holiday then. The hotel is cheap. But I will meet her."

"You might be glad of her. And you'll ring us reverse charges if anything goes wrong. Anything could happen there."

"Nothing will go wrong. I know what I'll be doing."

"Oh, have you a lot planned? I thought you were just going to let things happen."

"Oh, yes. No, no. Just a few things. There's a lot to see, I believe."

Valerie batted her eyelids. *Well, if you don't want to tell me, keep it to yourself, see if I care. It can't be all that exciting, I'm sure.* Unlike her fiancé, without the ring, she had an instinct about subterfuge.

Queuing up in the passport line during the day put Maud among the travellers. And at night she read her secret library stash. She was determined to know as much as possible about the workings of this death industry. She sometimes wished that she really was going on a proper holiday. No matter, next time maybe. She changed her telephone bill from itemised status. Malachy might, in his good brotherliness, open it while she was away, in order to pay it. She had tried refusing his offer to check the flat, but the refusal had sounded sharp, so she had given him a key. The calls would make strange reading. Ten to the same number over a period of three days. Ten, because the man she needed was never at his desk. It wouldn't take that many calls to book a room in a hotel. He knew a night telephonist who would oblige with tracing numbers. If he didn't notice, Valerie would, if he happened to leave it lying about. The number was that of the Anti-Capital Punishment Section, Amnesty International, New York. She bought a new case. The travel bag section of Roches Stores sizzled with the deferred excitement of people about to devolve themselves from their proper lives. She packed the case in instalments, pushing it underneath her bed after each satisfied visit.

"Have you got everything?" they hummed at her, before they left her house. "Passport, tickets, money?"

The old mantra that makes travellers smile.

"Yes, yes."

At the airport they buzzed around her with care, making a ceremony of the move forward in the check-in queue, investing the escalator ride up to the restaurant with the importance of a unique journey of its own.

"No, no, no, you sit down, I'll get it. Would you like a pastry?"

"No, thanks."

"Anything else? Would you like anything else?"

"No, no, coffee will be fine."

Maud lit a cigarette and longed to tell Malachy. But to do that now would be unfair, and, having decided this at the end of her ten long weak seconds, she wanted to get away from them fast. Valerie kissed her at the departure gate like a French woman, twice, which saved her putting too much feeling into the one. Malachy hugged her as if she was stepping away from him for ever.

"I'm only going for ten days," Maud said, with a sound caught halfway between a sniffle and a smile.

She bought cigarettes in the duty free and a bottle of Baileys for Valerie's cousin. The top had stuck on the last one of those she had purchased. She had had to use the bread knife on it, ruined the serrated edge completely. She made her way to the boarding gate, filed on in shuffling movements, strapped herself into her seat and sighed at the finality of the clasp snap. It was then that the captain said seven and a half hours.

* * *

Nothing, not even her preoccupation, could take away from the pleasure of her first sight of New York. From the aeroplane she could see needles of buildings, growing stalagmites out of the earth. She was a cartographer in the sky. She couldn't wait to be down among them. Her exit from the airport was brisk and much more easily accomplished than she had expected. The road outside was strewn with film-set cars. The air was hot, buzzing with noise and smells. She found the bus, still surprised at how easy it was. The bus stuttered through traffic towards her first ground view of Manhattan, where the post-card buildings straightened themselves under a red ball of set-ting sun. She grabbed the arm of the passenger next to her and gasped out loud, "My God, it's beautiful."

The hotel was adequate, clean sheets. And Maud slept again.

* * *

The noise of the morning was continuous. She showered, dressed, had breakfast, took a taxi, conscious of all her move-ments. But although she was on a mission, for that's all she could call it now, she noticed as many single things as she pos-sibly could. It would be hard to concentrate on the minutiae of her search while all her senses were being so entertained.

The man who came down to speak to the Irish visitor who wanted to know more about capital punishment in the Unit-ed States was in his early thirties, thin, tanned and easygoing. They chatted about place names while fleeing up in the eleva-tor. In the room he handed her a bundle of stapled pages.

"I'm sorry, I have to rush out for fifteen minutes. I'll leave you with these. They're the lists. We have them divided: men, women, juveniles, innocent, already executed. Now, with the men we have some sub-divisions: age, colour, colour of victim, number of victims, age when found guilty. You'll have every-thing you need there. The next person up is this one, we think."

He took the papers back from her for a moment and worked his finger up and down through the pages.

"Yes, this one, number 438 here. So I'll leave you to it. I'll be back and we can have coffee then."

He waved briefly and left the room. Maud stood firmly in her spot, shaking, holding the names of these people, afraid to sit down in case the act of moving a muscle might bring bad luck on them, speed their final dates. It was as if she had dynamite in her hands, as if one wrong move would trip the voltage on a chair, jab a needle in. Her hands shook, her face went cold, her mouth quivered then dried, as if she was going to descend into some kind of arid dark spasm. She wished the young man would come back.

But there were office noises here. Five people hurried in looking for a table to have a meeting, excused themselves to her, hurried out looking for a spare room. Maud relaxed a little, sat down, spread the pages out in front of her. She scanned the numbers, found Xavier's, then started to read the names. They were so precious, those names. Oh God, someone had named them. And there were six Harrys.

CHAPTER 11

MAUD SPENT THE next few days amassing information about her subject, as she now called it. It was a funny place, this death row. It didn't have the normal proximity necessary to make it a row; thousands heaped upon thousands of miles separated some parts of it from others. Nor did it have the physical likenesses of, say, a row of green beans or a row of skittles. It wasn't a corridor, although it might be a collection of solitary cells. It was instead a state of being. The row could come from an imaginary line of people waiting for the end. Or the line of people from her childhood awoken from their sleep to face judgment and banishment on the last day. In catechism class Maud hadn't imagined too many people being picked for heaven. Certainly she hadn't seen herself as being one of them.

She read about executioners and men who invented machines for killing, diligently doing their market research before embarking on the hard sell. She read their PR and even an advertisement for the sale of a used electric chair. The tone of her belief in the innate goodness of human beings was being lowered, but only the tone, because, despite appearances, she was an optimistic sort of person. She could conjure merriness. She could revert easily to a time before knowing hard things. She could remember innocence as it had been and school friends sloping to school, and she wouldn't have minded meeting any of them again to exchange chit chat and check their alibis for how they had spent their years. Mundane things would be best to hear.

She went slowly through her reading, concentrating on the old and the young, imagining their faces, their frames, their walks, as if that would let her know them and as if they would be better off because of that. It wasn't arrogance that made her think this, it was merely naivety. She was often sad but also often hopeful, or at least wishful. Her pursuit was the construction of a conversation with Harry. That was the whole point of the exercise. And she reminded herself of that continuously. By the time she returned the lists she had got used to unpalatable facts.

On the street again, the sky startled her, more because she remembered to notice it, patiently stretching above the tall buildings, than because it had any particular properties. A warm wind occasionally broke out. It must be rattling things, but she couldn't hear above the noise.

She wondered what she should feel about the things she now knew. Idly wondered, because procrastination was the clearest emotion that she actually did feel. She wondered if procrastination was an emotion. Wouldn't it be better to leave things be until she was back in her own bed, underneath her own duvet, that she still called a continental quilt, with her own thin bedside lamp blazing? Wouldn't it be better to let the facts rumble around with themselves until only the important ones stuck? Concentrating on details, however comforting, was a distraction. It postponed the crisis that would come when she would have to face the fact that she needed a fundamental plan, that she wanted to do something. Prevarication would be no good then. Making comparisons like a philosopher could go on for ever, but would be ultimately unsatisfying. Trying to hang on to the mere periphery of her thoughts would become impossible. In the meantime, she deserved some light relief.

She went to a bar and sat alone, terribly pleased with herself for having the nerve. It was an Irish bar, which made it easier, but she wasn't about to labour that too much. She didn't want to take away from her bravery. She contrived her way into a conversation, because she was not without her own wiles.

"Are you on vacation?"

"Yes and no. I'm doing a little research for my thesis, but I must get around to some socialising before I go back."

The lie slipped out smoothly and seemed to be accepted by the three women at the table. She engaged in five minutes' conversation, happy to be chatting. "I've got to go now to meet some people. It was nice meeting you."

"Good luck with your thesis."

She could, of course, copy any manners; she could distort with the best of them. Before she extricated herself she had got an invitation to a party. She went to another bar, another Irish bar. "Corner of 28th and Lexington," she said to the taxi driver, brimming with confidence. She had another wine but wasn't able to stretch out the good feeling to last the length of the drink. This bar was more anxious than the last one. Customers came and went rapidly, putting chunky big glasses to their lips and emptying shorts quickly. Only two men who were there when she came in were still there when she left. They lifted their eyebrows to each other as she reached the door.

Once outside she felt warmed by a new excitement and decided to try one more bar, not an Irish one. But she would only have one drink. A person had to be careful. A person could stumble on danger, not having seen sight nor sign of it a minute before. Danger was like that; it could happen suddenly. A murder could happen in a minute.

The new place was an American bar, which is only proper in America. It was quite full, but she found herself a seat that faced the window. She involved herself in the liturgy of smoking, then opened a book to read. It was an English thriller, where the murder was always neat and discreet and the perpetrator came to no more harm than being led handcuffed into a station. She lifted her head occasionally and looked at the opening door, squinting, as if she was waiting for someone, occasionally checking her watch. The person obviously didn't turn up, and she made little preparations to depart, all sudden gestures that alerted the man beside her. If she had had gloves, she wouldn't have had them on before he spoke.

"Are you on vacation?"

How the hell was it that everyone knew?

"Yes," she said this time, and, "I'm afraid that my friend and I have mixed up our bars, so I'd better go soon to our hotel."

"How long are the two of you staying?"

He shuffled into the few minutes that were left.

"Another five days. Beautiful city. We love it."

"You're Irish, aren't you?"

"Yes."

"From near the Blarney Stone?"

Jesus.

"No, not exactly."

"My name is Gerard," he said. "We're having a party here tomorrow night if you and your friend would like to come."

He was hoping that she would slip on her remarks and let him know the sex of her friend, not that that was any guarantee of anything. It couldn't have been better for Maud. She could now leave, and if she wanted to come tomorrow night her friend could have had to go home suddenly, to a funeral perhaps, and they could only get one seat on the plane. God, this was a great city. You could say anything you liked. Out on the street she stumbled slightly, reaching for the ground with her feet as if it was moving away from her.

* * *

Maud went to the party and told her lies. Gerard was bright with solicitousness. References like the Blarney Stone were not fallen into again; it must have been an accident of awkwardness. Early in the evening he asked her if she would like to come to a weekend party in Kutsher's Country Club, high up in the Catskill Mountains. The place where the Jewish people used to summer, throw their wit about together, in an effort to forget their rotten pasts, just for the holidays.

"There's a huge Irish music jamboree on, I'm sure you'll love it. My company has a serious interest in the business end of things."

"I see," she said.

"Oh, but I do like the music as well," he said quickly, trying to cover any crassness that she might have imagined.

"I'll bet," she said, then smiled, thinking that he might indeed like it better than she did herself, because in all honesty she'd never paid that much attention to it, had never found a way into it, other than a primal one which linked her to the beat. He turned away to talk to a woman who had just sashayed into their corner; there was no other way to describe her arrival. He left Maud with the invitation, allowing her time to say no, but judging, correctly, that the arrival of the woman might edge her into saying yes. By the time he turned back again she had her mind made up. Harry had, after all, been a fiddler.

"Yes, that would be nice."

"Great," he smiled, his eyes becoming a tribute to small pleasures. Because she didn't want to appear too anxious, she insisted on making her own way back to the hotel. He liked the way she said taxi. Back in her room, she thought that the trouble about doing without sex was that you had to do without its accessories, consenting telephone calls, the sound of low oily voices and being held tight in grasps that weren't hygienic.

* * *

Kutsher's Country Club was evening coming on. Maud and Gerard took their belongings to the check-in desk. She carried her bags, one of them over her shoulder, the one she'd bought in Roches; the other, a new black match bought in Maceys, in her hand. She was alive with embarrassment as she allowed him to check in. She didn't know whether they would share a room, but knew that if he asked for two singles that she could cope, being well used to solitude and a drought of touch. She looked down the satisfyingly long corridor. The smell of chlorine from the swimming pool invaded the front hall, adding a headiness to her long moment of delicious waiting. He turned his head.

"Number 348, it's on the third floor. Is that all right with you?"

She would have liked the sophistication that she was feigning to have been solidly obvious, but instead she laughed out loud, a gurgling kind of laugh. "Fine, absolutely fine," she said. He also laughed.

Over the weekend they ate kosher steamed food, the chefs not being prepared to change a lifetime custom for the sake of a fleeting party of a thousand gentiles. They shared round tables with men who looked as if they were still in Leitrim, but who wore the comfortable wealth and staidness of a Milwaukee life like a badge of high honour, and women with engagement rings bought in Hardogan's of Galway, minded, loved and polished to pristine through the years of Irish dances, small babies, children graduating, two in apprenticeships and one in college.

"Where are you from?" a breakfast companion opened up the morning conversation, after the first sip of orange juice.

She wondered what would be for dinner. Did eggs affect anything? Or was it just dairy and meat? And was it true about the three hour rule?

"Dublin," she said.

"I know, I know," he replied, with a hint of annoyance, "but where are you from now?"

"Dublin," she said.

"Oh, I see."

He turned away from her to speak to one of his own.

Maud and Gerard dropped in and out of the various music sessions that were taking place in all available corners. They watched Irish American girls kick their feet up to ceilings and the men prance delighted steps that shone with noise. They watched a Galway man, here for the weekend, face up a solo *sean-nós* with an Appalachian dancer whose hips swung her skirts into a halo of their own. Maud drank wine, smiled sometimes as if her face might crack, and shook her head at the thought of everything that could be good in a world suspended above real life. They walked along the corridor to the lift, watching the masseuses of new time work on the strained necks and wrists of marathon music players. They went to bed to the distant uplifting sounds of fiddles matching note for note with brisk flutes, leaving no time for the air between to fall into confusion.

As they drove back to New York, through the beauty that belongs exclusively to the beginning fall, one almost too good to be true, Maud savoured her aching body and the smell of perfect time.

"When will I see you again?" Gerard asked, before they hit the New York State highway. Maud sighed.

"You will. Definitely you will, but we'll have to wait a little while."

Because this weekend had been one of such enormous intimacy without the usual requisite knowledge of background, he said, "OK, that's fine," wondering perhaps if she had a husband and if he had a right to ask. He suspected not, so he didn't.

CHAPTER 12

MAUD WASN'T SURE what she had accomplished by her visit to New York, but knew that it had been a necessary first step. She couldn't be sure because she didn't know where this hunting would take her. She took sick leave in order to visit Mountjoy Prison. It would have seemed too gauche to take a day's holiday. She made the phone calls to the prison from a public phone. The first polite man, called Keith Darwin, didn't know how many women were hanged or when the last one was executed. Maud had used the question as an angle to lead her into this conversation. Yes, the chief knew the name of the last man. He had murdered a nurse in Limerick. Only the other day the chief himself had been talking to the prison officer who specialled him, retired now of course. The man's mother had been in the night before the execution and complained, on her way out, that he had a terrible cold and a sore throat.

"Mothers will always find something to worry about."

Maud agreed with this incongruous statement. He told her the address to which she should write her letters requesting permission for a visit.

"Then make an appointment and I'll show you around, certainly." He called it the gallows room. "It's soon going to be made into a museum."

Well, that's good, Maud thought. *Things don't happen in museums.*

The second phone call was answered by a less reverential young woman. She could afford to be; she would not have known anyone who would have sat with a man the night before his hanging. She called it the hang house. "There's a woman here who says she's been on before, she wants to visit the hang house."

"Here, let me speak to her." The polite man came back on the line. "Come to the main gate, ask for me personally, don't say that you're going to visit the hang. . . eh, the gallows room."

What would she wear? Would she put on make-up? Would a skirt be better than trousers?

She wrote the required letters on a Saturday. It was like requesting planning permission. She asked to visit on Wednesday the twenty-third, a sort of anniversary date. She didn't admit her relationship to a hanged man, merely outlined a general interest in historical research. She worried about backup proof from a relevant institution and was disproportionally relieved when it wasn't requested. Disproportionate to what wasn't clear to her.

She waited at the number 22 bus-stop, knowing vaguely that it went in the right direction. She had no intention of specifying her destination. Instead she asked a woman standing at the bus-stop, "What number goes near the Mater Hospital?"

"A number 22 would do, this one coming now."

"Thank you."

The prison officer had suggested that she come at lunchtime when the men would be locked up eating. He thought that they might be sensitive about people visiting the gallows room. Maud sat in the waiting room with several women: mothers, wives, one of them young enough to be a girlfriend. She was afraid to look at them. Being practised in the faculties appropriate to this predicament, the women exchanged weather comments. Maud tried to get her tongue around something meteorological. She couldn't spit it out. The women dragged on their cigarettes as if they were lungs working on their outsides.

"Miss Mannering?"

Here we go, she thought, *too late to back out now.* She tiptoed behind him, as if there were many babies having naps behind the doors. Keith Darwin chattered on as if all this was normal. They had now gone through three doors that didn't really fit the word door; there were no connotations of opening attached to them. A crowd of officers noisily flocked past them, the lines of keys attached to their bodies clanging out of rhythm. So many keys they could chafe their legs. Various officers saluted her guide.

"Chief."

"Hello, Paul."

"Chief."

"Hello, Brendan."

"Chief."

"Hello, Jack."

"Now we'll go this way."

Thank God he wasn't a quiet man. He would keep the talking up until she got her dry mouth around her questions. He led her to the gallows room, a stone disused outhouse hidden from all view. They went down the steps, the chief turned the key in the steel door, and they entered the musty damp rectangle. So this was it. By shuffling uncomfortably a few steps forward, Maud was standing underneath the trap door. The two halves of the heavy wooden door hung harmlessly each side of the hole. There was no swing in them, but you could hear the echo of that final noise. Above her, Maud could see the upper region, the sturdy beams in the ceiling. It could be any old harmless ceiling. A fluorescent light shone brightness about them. It was like a sun from where she stood. At eye level opposite her there was an inside door and above was a sort of stage. The door led on to a platform, with a railing which stepped down to her feet.

"That's the door the doctor and the priest came through. After."

The chief wanted to speak about after. His eyes looked to the ground, an ordinary man who would lower his voice in a graveyard, take off his hat to a passing hearse. Maud looked up again. She would not imagine her mother's uncle falling through, dangling before his God. She knew that it was possible to put a moratorium on one's imagination. She would not concentrate on her mother's uncle, or indeed on any other man, or woman. She would simply observe and listen. Later she would fit this into some private memorial.

"Well, there would be a number of people here — the governor, the chaplain, the doctor, a prison visitor, the officers who had been with him the night before, a prisoner or two. I suppose they would get time off for helping. And the tradesmen, of course. It was a precise thing. You would need tradesmen to do it right, you see."

They both looked up again. There was a lot of looking up and looking down and looking at each other, so they could imagine themselves in a different room.

"The measuring would have been done first. A man would have to fall his own length. The safety key would be removed. When the doors opened, the remains fell."

No matter that they were not the remains of a man until some seconds after the door opened.

"The executioner would stand on the planks, of course."

Of course. What was she doing here, going through these mathematics?

"And the carpenter would be there, about where you're standing now."

The carpenter, of course.

"There were weights on both sides of the door. The weights would stop short of the ground."

Of course.

"And you see the padding on the doors, that was to stop them banging too hard on the wall."

Of course. It would never do to have unnecessary noise.

"And then the chaplain would perform the last rites, and the doctor would examine him."

The chief kept another moment's silence.

"There would be a period of time before the prisoners took him down."

Of course.

"Now we'll go upstairs. But be careful, a lot of this floor is rotten now."

Upstairs was airier. There was a lot of rusting equipment. Maud went near the open door, too near for the chief's liking. Here would be where the two feet of a live man felt their last weight. He would never see down like she could. Did her uncle look at the walls? Could she go now?

Chief Darwin then locked the doors of that room and led her out into the part of the prison proper which joined that room. The place of the man's last walk.

"Here are what were the death cells." One of them was now a toilet. "There would have been the man in here, and two officers. Small really for three of them."

The officers' jobs would have been to ensure that the prisoner did not cheat the hangman. He would have been led through this corridor. The corridor was now a television viewing area. Chairs were neatly placed in rows awaiting evening watching. Did the present-day inmates know that this was part of the last walk? Had a sensitive one among them ever gone off television? The chief led Maud down the corridor where the occasional prisoner had had his door opened and was emerging from the cell with his lunch plate cleaned spotless. There would be no fussy pushing about of food here, unless a man was heartsick and couldn't even keep soup down. Some men nodded politely to her. They might not have seen her. She was trying not to be seen and trying certainly not to be a woman.

It was hard to know how to do that. Did you fold your arms under your breasts so that they didn't protrude, or did that make them more noticeable? And did the absence of arms swinging by your side make the roundness of your hips more obvious? She strode, eyes down, looking at Chief Darwin's heels, which was why she nearly bumped into a prisoner.

"Oh, gosh, I'm sorry."

"Oh, don't mind, miss."

The prisoner beamed and winked at her. It was a wink that, in the circumstances, could crack a heart open, as if it had been hit by fork lightning.

"Now, Harry," Chief said, not too harshly.

"Harry! Did you say his name was Harry?"

"Yes, why?"

"Oh, no why, no why. My father's name is Harry," she lied, "that's all, and it's not so usual a name."

She still occasionally used "is" about her father.

In the chief's office, he showed Maud old photographs. She might like to see these details for her research. Oh yes, her research.

"Look how the uniform has changed; look at the old caps. When that photograph was taken, you had to have high buttons. Unless you were the governor, of course."

Chief Darwin was throbbing with information, glad of this hiatus away from hanging. Other men with keys came and went, some to open cupboard doors to get the cigarettes for D wing, some to get small unnamed packages for A wing, some to banter and ask, "What's a woman doing in here with us?" And to say, "Oh," when being told the reason for her visit. The shape of the Oh exposed who thought that the hang house should still be in use and who was embarrassed by the history of his job. A flash of an argument erupted about one photograph of a group of prisoners. Was it grey for sentenced and blue for remand when that was taken? Grey, no blue, blue, no grey. The next one caused no problems: those lines of men in military formation doing exercises, all in suits, were the politicos. Way back then.

"Politicals, not politicos," said the one startlingly good-looking man among them.

"Right," the chief said, wishing to break up this gaggle before his men disgraced themselves by straightening their backs or by falling into snorts. "We're off to see the chapel."

And so they went. The door was painted lime-green gloss.

"A condemned man would come through the chaplain's entrance and would sit here. Are you RC?"

"Well, yes," Maud said, not wishing to go into the finer details of mature agnosticism.

"Then you'll know that pre-Vatican the altar would have been this way. So the priest could see the man. The other prisoners couldn't see him, nor he them. It made it easier on everyone."

"Not for the man, surely. Would he not have liked to have seen friendly faces?"

"I don't think you realise, not all prisoners are friendly. Some, yes some, and there are murderers, too, who are not bad men. Oh yes, definitely, without a doubt. But we cannot care about them, we just care for them."

He rattled his keys, annoyed at having said too much. Maud knew that if there was a God, he was in prison chapels.

"I'll show you the book."

Maud followed the chief again. Her clothes were getting sticky. The chief flourished his hand like a tour guide new to the job.

"In the old days before that wall was built, the prisoners could see the lines of women waiting to visit."

Not much changes; fewer men always did that particular unbearable duty. The women would tell them when they went home. There wouldn't have been a coffee shop.

"And for the politicals, there would sometimes be carriages passing there. Women standing up waving at windows."

The book was hardbacked and lined, like that of a district midwife. Name. Address. Medical opinion of the cause of death. Verdict of the Inquest Jury. Observations.

"The inquest jury?" Maud said, the surprise of it making her voice loud. "But surely it was obvious."

"Oh no, some men died of natural causes, and they're in this book, too."

Maud flicked the pages surreptitiously to find Harry Tavey.

> Medical Opinion of Cause of Death: *Dislocation and fracture of third cervical vertebra.*
> Verdict of Jury: *Harry Tavey died in Mountjoy Prison on the 23/4/41 from fractured dislocation of third vertebra, the result of judicial hanging.*
> Signed: *Coroner.*
> Observation: *Executed. Remains interred within the precincts of the prison, rear of hospital.*

Maud read it again, trying not to look too interested in that one entry.

And so the grave. There was one cross over a multiple grave

for patriots. "Relatives visit here at times. The cross was erected in 1966."

The chief shuffled Maud away from this edifice.

"And here is where the ordinary hanged men were buried. After the inquest, the coffins would have been brought out to this place."

He pointed to a thin strip of grass huddling against the granite walls. A miserable thin strip of grass, no gravestones, no names, no surround where a person could kneel one knee to pray. The top end of it was being concreted, made into a footpath that would join a new extension. Could there possibly be dead men under that concrete? Couldn't they at least have preserved the hinterland of this measly bit of earth and let their sorrow come up with the grass? Maud would have liked to have had a camera with her. She would have liked to photograph this spot, as an emigrant might line up an old headstone in the viewer.

The chief joined his hands behind his back. His uniform with its three stripes on the label was neat and spotless. His radio hung comfortably on him, like a woman's shoulder bag. He bent his head, perhaps thinking that he would like a better funeral than had ever happened here. Maud bent her head, too, and kept the tears well behind her eyes, giving her the sort of headache that comes with eating cold ice cream. She heard the keys rattle and was not sorry. This was the last moment here.

CHAPTER 13

THE DEMONSTRATION WAS to be held on a Saturday, soon, outside the American Embassy at 3 o'clock, to protest against an execution. Maud first saw the poster on her way to work. She was late and was trying to control her impatience when the word execution loomed off the poster. She tried to ignore the information, then glanced at it again. *That has nothing to do with me. How could that have anything to do with me?* Last year she had known little of these things and thought even less. But the word was in the car with her, sitting there familiarly. She must be going mad. Yet it was true that she had sometimes wanted to go to a demonstration, any demonstration. She had never done so, because those things were for other people, people not to be looked at as the bus or the car passed slowly, as the guards swung their arms in

an attempt to get drivers to move on, in an attempt not to let
the entire road come to a standstill. But inevitably drivers
slowed slower than necessary as they do at accidents' time. You
could look at the placards from a bus, squinting your eyes —
What's it about? — and then some passenger would make a
very quiet hah noise, which threw a security blanket around
those people who did not want to know. Because the noise was
so quiet it could be ignored. But if Maud had ever seen the
crowd on the street and what they looked like, she surely
couldn't have wanted to throw her lot in with them?

And yet at work that day she thought about demonstrators. They would be people who concentrated on the perils of
others, people who were saddened by wrongs but galvanised
by a belief that standing in cold and wind, shouting, holding
home painted cardboard banners or long pieces of material
painted in red made a difference. Changed things. They would
be people with well-informed innocence. Maybe. Because in
truth, as Maud struggled with the paperwork of her day, she
knew that she didn't know what those people would be like.
Or what had made them different from her. Could you go to
a gathering like that on your own? Would there be bundles of
people all knowing each other hugging into conversation, and
would she be left standing alone, with eyes examining the
ground? Would someone she knew see her from a passing bus?
Because if someone she knew saw her from the street, she
could walk through the demonstrators as if she was heading
down the road, but a bus would be different. She wouldn't see
the people seeing her.

What the heck, she would go. What did she have to lose?
No one would know — only the people who would be there,

SKIN OF DREAMS • 91

and in the scheme of her life they didn't matter. Of course, the trouble was she was afraid that they did matter to her now, at least as much as her ordinary friends, her office neighbours, her coffee drinking companions, her picture going mates, the people she met in bars. Those other people, those demonstration goers? No one likes a conscience. A conscience rumbles away, jabbing at comfort. It doesn't get paid. It gets highly praised in obituaries, but definitely not paid, and never invited to the A list parties. People do not like its voice, it has too little obedience in it. A young man had stolen a car from the flat next door to Valerie, Malachy told her. Malachy and Valerie saw him do it and went to the guards. He had cycled ten miles to get it; he had had his eye on it.

"How enterprising," Maud muttered.

"What did you say?"

"Nothing."

"A fairly noisy nothing."

Maud wouldn't go to the guards now. Her secret had thrown a shadow on the law.

The demonstrators did not all look the same. They stamped their feet to shoo away the cold. They clapped their gloves together and talked to Maud as if they knew her. The whole thing took two hours. Pointless? Perhaps. The three people beside her were going to the Waterloo, or Searsons maybe, for a hot whiskey.

"Would you like to come?"

"No, thanks."

She didn't want to push herself too far. But when she got home, she felt satisfied with herself. Not smug, nothing as outlandishly disproportionate as that. Still, she was now someone who could move out beyond her own needs. She had heard the high difficult note of a just demand being carried like a wild swan's perfect pitch through a frosty morning. She was not, any more, a person who wouldn't give you the drop off a pin or muck from a turnip.

CHAPTER 14

MAUD HAD A nap on a Saturday afternoon and woke in a nasty cocoon of low blood sugar. Her mother would have had a Marie biscuit with jam. She had better do the same thing, not knowing a different remedy. There were unusually quiet workmen in the house next door, tapping tools like dancers with amateur rhythms, or prisoners sending messages through the plumbing. That must have been the noise which had made the ticking clock in her dream. She looked out the window to untie herself from it. The afternoon was completely bright, no dark shades in the sky warning people not to take too much for granted. It would be a good day to take decisions. And there were lots to be taken.

Should she go to a psychotherapist? The thought of it had occasionally fascinated her, the pure selfish pleasure of it. To go before now might have suggested that she needed to go, but now she had a good excuse — grief. That would be the opening line, a thing that had stymied her every other time she had thought about it. Because she had known that once the embarrassment of the first line was over, she would have raced through her story like a child approaching the last ten skips. Now she had the line: "My parents were killed in a car crash some time ago." No, she would say the actual date. And he would say, "How do you feel?" and she would spend some time trying to explain the unexplainable, but would give up and take a side road up her own life and talk about her work and how ordinary it was, and how little satisfaction she got from it, but how dependent upon it she was, for fear that she would stay in bed all day. And how they kept promoting her and how she didn't understand why. And how she was friends with her co-workers only because they were her co-workers and it seemed appropriate. And then she would say that if her parents hadn't died she wouldn't know what she now knew about her granduncle, who seemed closer, like an uncle, with no extra generation removed. And how knowing him and his life had given her some purpose, one that she had never had before. But the man would then explain, although he wasn't supposed to, that she was just a fighter, a survivor, trying to deal with the negative.

If she went to a psychotherapist, she could think about herself and not the broader world. She could stop being obsessional. But what was obsession? People wanted to own apartments with stick-on balconies. People wanted to be in love. They wanted to have more money than they could spend. They wanted to have moments of brilliant light alone. And then share it afterwards. They wanted to have their cake and eat it. New cake that they couldn't even name. They wanted to be thinner than they were. Her mother had agreed to have her photograph taken in summertime. But Maud knew that she was lining herself up, against the light, hoping and believing that the camera would make her look like she had once been, before she had had twins, when her thighbones would have been visible through her dress. Her mother had not wanted to be alive, she had merely wanted to be thinner, as if being thinner would mean she had no secret.

Decision number two. What to do about drink. Should she give it up? Last weekend she had drunk too much — no, really she should admit this properly, she had been on a complete bender. The way young men or builders do. The Friday night had been unexpected, a night for falling into. She had agreed to have a drink after work, and there was just some enormous relief attached to the whiff of the second one. She already had her excuse for a third, and then the buying of her own round, and then the starting of the next round. Her head was filled with a melodious noise. She swallowed every single thing that was a component part of the worry of her life, and by allowing these things passage down her throat, they disappeared, rather than settling like bile in her stomach. The paranoia of her thoughts melted, as surely as if boiling water had been sprayed on snow. This place was too good to leave. The merry-go-round of mutual satisfaction caught them all, as surely as if they were being sucked into the eye of a tornado. There were things said that should not have been said, but the trouble was that she couldn't remember what they were. And her extra trouble was that the other drinkers would remember.

They were men with practice, better body mass for absorption and feet on a steadier ground.

And worse than words had happened. She had gone home with a man. Not even one of the men with whom she had been drinking. She had left suddenly, because she felt herself about to be propositioned. She couldn't remember now by which of the company. Although they were less drunk than she was, they were still taken aback by her sudden departure. They didn't argue too much about lifts home, nor taxies, partly because of the surprise of her donned coat and partly because they remembered that Maud was known for her sharp, almost jagged, exits. But out on the street she had begun to wobble and had decided to have coffee in a café that smoldered with yellow light. Maud couldn't, or didn't want to, remember how she had got talking to the man. She could recall a build-up of sensation in her body, and common sense warning her, and then a delicious surrendering of wisdom. She went with him to his flat, even worse, more dangerous, than if she had brought him to her own place. And after, when he had fallen contentedly asleep, she had slipped out into the street, like a man might. She could not remember how she had got a taxi. The following morning she had been terrified by the danger she had courted. It was not that she disapproved of herself going to bed with a man. It was that she knew that she should use some reasonable precaution, any precaution. Yes, of course, one had to have some bad luck to meet a nightmare, but bad luck was not as scarce as she wanted to make herself believe the next morning. If only she had been more sober, they could have absolved themselves by preambling with guilt, and then they could have dismissed it. Doctors, mind people, ordinary sensible people, and the police, would all have something to say about a night like that.

She asked Malachy if he thought that she drank with too little caution.

"You have to make that decision yourself. Otherwise you'll ring me up sometime from a pub and say that I am putting restrictions on you."

In other words, he thought yes. But then he said, "Look, it's what you do."

So there was no decision to be made. The losses of not having a drink again were too colossal to be contemplated. If she did go to a psychotherapist, she would leave that night out.

Decision number three. Should she have an affair? Why call it an affair? She wasn't married. Was she supposing that the man would be, and why would she do that? And if she was doing that, why? She did not want to get involved with an actually available man at this precise time because she couldn't love anyone in this state. Well, that was clear enough, the psychotherapist would agree. But a person has to get out of their town sometimes. She had certainly disappeared off the globe of her street the other night. But only after she had drunk herself out of her skull, or drunk her skull off, whatever way a young dissatisfied man would say it. Or a middle-aged woman with a side view who was drowning in her own laugh.

Some people want romance so that they can live it, and others want it so that they can forget. The way Maud felt at the moment, she could sweep it under the darkest corner and happily get into a truck driver's cabin with never a thought for his wife or children. Not a dangerous truck driver, of course. The trouble could come in not being able to tell until afterwards.

So, back to a proper relationship, a proper going out and stay-ing in. But if love, for want of a better word — she was, after all, only imagining — if love could make people as confluent and then as nasty as it did, why bother? Still it was possible that she could meet a man, why not? Other women did. But she tripped into a half hour of "what ifs". Her balance of potential worries was in the black, so she could call on one of them any-time that things were going Jim-dandy. The whole precarious-ness of it all was giving her the pip.

Decision number four. Had it ever crossed her mind to have a child? No one ever asks that question because it is too rude. One tries not to ask it, even of oneself. So Maud asked, in the safety of a late afternoon, when nothing could be done about it one way or the other. It was apparently a natural thing to do. But imagine the huge disappointment that children could turn into. Disappointment presupposes expectations, and expectation is necessary to the parent who must recom-pense herself for the sacrifice. Disappointment has to have comparison, so to whom would one compare one's children? And, achievement is such a fickle thing, a person wouldn't know whether they were right to be disappointed or not. A Civil Service job, considered boring now, might be a de luxe career in ten years time, powdered with the allure of power. Or the service industry might become sexy. Or teaching might inspire love. What if she had a dyslexic child and didn't realise it until it was too late? What if her child died before she did, was killed in an accident, say? And what if her child was a boy and hated his mother when he grew up, particularly at the times that he had no girlfriend. Malachy had. Snapped things from their mother's hand, ignored her civil ordinary questions;

and then when he did have a girlfriend, it was hard to figure out who he was in love with, her or his mother.

Maud's perceived children were always grown up. She knew that this was not a good start, that there were things to be gone through before that: the torture of broken sleep to be endured, babysitters to be procured. Malachy said that he wanted children. It was a clear and simple thing with him, and when it would happen, Maud touched the leg of her chair, he would fold it into his life as one would a welcome guest who has come to stay for longer than normal.

Decision number five. Should she go away on a real holiday, stand outside travel agent windows, jot down place names previously scoffed at, compare bargains from shop to shop, apply for leave, and then, pleasure of pleasures, book the trip? Get date and times marked down on a ticket? And should she go with one other person, that woman in the next office whose laugh was loose, or two people, that woman and their shared typist who would organise them into the ground and rub her hands at evening's end with the glee of all the miles she had made them walk, all the monuments she had made them see? And the receptionist, a lovely woman, lovely meaning — my God, so all enveloping, untaut, good. An impossible aspiration. Or should she go alone? That would give her more freedom to do the things that she might be ashamed of. Enjoy, but be ashamed of. Still, that could be lonely. Maybe the other women would let her slide off. Maybe they would all slide off together and keep the secret.

Decision number six. Should she just go to the pictures? But all the pictures, or films, that she had seen this year had been called epics. She actually preferred the word movies, images that move, but pictures was OK, too. Films were too equipment based. She wasn't that fond of epics, stories that took one part of a life and made it much bigger than the others. If you did that with physical parts, the actors would have overgrown noses, and rugby players would have ears and lips like tyres. There was no irony in these epics, no allegories. There may have been a room from where film makers went to pick up images. Otherwise, how could there have been so many skinny women with perfect, bland faces picking petals or baptising children while shots went off, and how could so many men have been thinking about machinery as they soared into lovemaking?

The pictures she had seen this year had made honest local enthusiasm about facts into a garish thing, a souvenir that could be bought and put on a mantelpiece, anywhere in the world. And going to the movies in the afternoon was for Connemara men on a Saturday in London, trying to put off the hour of the first drink. Or for bailed criminals awaiting trial, men who knew for certain that they were going down this time.

Yes, there were a lot of decisions to be made. To say no is to say yes. "No, I will not think about this," is "Yes, I will think about something more comfortable." We're supposed to say yes these days, yes to everything. To say no is a perversity. Yet Maud liked no having that status. It was better than if saying no had a smug sound: "Oh, my dear, no, of course I don't smoke/drink/go to bed with strangers."

There were too many decisions to be made. Maud had a bath. She would see if Malachy was free. She would ask Malachy a thing or two.

CHAPTER 15

ON THE NIGHT of 20 November 1940, Harry Tavey made his way to the *céilí*. It would not have been a regular night out for him, but Nicholas Cantwell had asked him to play, and it was always best to oblige the person who had taught you your first tunes. And a bottle of stout or two, which the Keenans always gave, would be very welcome. A little stout went well with tunes, just a little. The bicycle ride was slow up the hills, the wheels reluctant to loosen their grasp on the frozen patches of the road. But after the hills, the going was easy. He had to switch on the flash lamp on the flat, so that he didn't ride into the potholes or splash his new trousers. They weren't exactly new, but were new to this level. They were the trousers of his last, recently replaced, suit. They had just been demoted to this sort of wear. Some of the potholes sported a veneer of thin ice. As Harry crackled over one, he could have sworn that he heard a shot. Probably the ice. But there was another one. A clear bang. *What an odd time for someone to be shooting. What could you see in this dark? You'd need lights at the back of your eyes. Shooting at rats maybe, but how could you see them?* When he got to the house there was already a steady lap of conversation, and some people were testing out steps. At least three women tried not to look at him. Two fathers wondered what the chances would be. Harry Tavey was a handsome man, a good worker and a nifty fiddler. It was also most likely that he would inherit a substantial farm of land. The rumbling excitement in the room put the shots out of his head; he had meant to remark upon them, meant to wonder with someone who could have been shooting at that hour and what.

Harry sat down on a seat, opened his fiddle case and bantered his way into the next reel. They played "The Cup of Tea" and "Peter Street", "The Skylark" and "Maud Miller", "The Stick across the Hob" and "Richard Brennan's". The dancers danced the Ballycommon set, the Cashel set, the Siege of Ennis and the Haymakers' jig. He should have told somebody about the shots. But what with one thing and the other, settling into a tune, sliding into the next, remembering notes, the tucking of his fiddle into a groove in his neck, the leaning of his head to one side as, at last, he could flow with the sound of long hours to come, he forgot. And every now and again, he allowed himself to think that he was being watched by the dancers, or at least one of them. It was a satisfying thing, and even if he had no nerve when it came to women, at least he could string airs together. If only he had the words, he certainly had the thoughts. But if a tune could be overdone, and it could, you can be sure words could, too. No rush, there was plenty of time. When the dance was over and after the woman had waited in vain as long as was decent, the musicians gathered their instruments and left the house. It was hard to leave the room, cosy now with the heat of the just finished dance evaporated from the middle of the floor but still hanging in the corners. On the cold cycle home, Harry heard the tunes. They had colours, black, white, red, purple, and they were still rhyming with the noise of feet beating. Even the frost could not kill the sound that tumbled in his ears for the first few miles, then slipped out to waft through the hedges, and across the fields, eventually sounding like distant clapping in the hills. He slept well.

In the morning he rose early to exercise his greyhounds and to get himself in working order before facing into a day's labour with his cousin, whose continuous cheerfulness could, in all honesty, be sometimes hard to take. It was better to have some solitude first. The music last night had never been dense, unlike the freezing cold this morning. He stepped out over the land, the greyhounds trotting in front of him on their leads. As he went from field to field, he took the opportunity to count his uncle's sheep. He also brought a straying bull, which had wandered on to a neighbouring farm, back into the field. At the end of the third field, his hounds now on the loose with no cattle in sight, Harry noticed that some of the bushes he had used to block a gap had been pushed aside. He climbed up, wondering how on earth that had happened, and then he saw, on the other side of the hedge, a body. It was a woman's body, and it appeared to be lifeless. Beside it sat a small black dog. The dog growled at Tavey, but that was the least of his worries at that moment. Harry swivelled on his heel and rushed home. He told both his uncle and his aunt, who were still in bed, of his discovery. He then left immediately to tell the guards. He told the guards that, because of the dog, he could not go near the body to check whether it was dead or whether the woman was asleep. He said that he knew that it was a woman because of her dress and her shoes. He did not say that he recognised it at once as that of his neighbour Moll Graney. He was not sure, never became sure, why he did not tell them this.

The doctor who examined Moll Graney found a cartridge wad wedged in her hair. Her coat had been torn, but the rest of her clothes were not damaged. Although the coat was buttoned, there was blood on its interior — an odd discovery, one whose significance and puzzlement was overlooked immediately. The doctor also believed that Moll had been shot in another place. He realised, by the position of her legs, that the body had been lifted, probably away from the place that she had been shot. He felt that her legs had been artificially placed one on top of the other and certainly were not in the stance of a woman who had been shot at that spot. But no matter what the doctor said, the cruel fact was that this body had been placed on this farm where Harry Tavey, whose movements were well known because of the exercising of his greyhounds, would inevitably find the body first thing in the morning. This simple fact hurled all suspicions directly at him.

Harry Tavey, his cousin, his aunt and uncle all gave rigorous descriptions of their movements. None of them led in any way to any evidence that anybody on this farm was involved in the murder of their neighbour. But suspicion is a gnawing thing, and the forces of law and order do like to believe that they will solve crime. It was an easier thing to do, to boil the suspicion to some kind of ready-made mix, so that this death would not hang over this place as a huge question mark for ever. Harry Tavey was brought to court. Harry Tavey was charged. There did not appear to be any evidence for this charge to remain. However, before the batting of too many eyelids, Harry Tavey was removed from his place to Mountjoy Prison and away from the useful petty rumbling of facts in his neighbourhood, the sound of which might in fact have thrown up another name, or at least thrown his out. In a newspaper report that Maud diligently read in the National Library, the history of events was recorded as if no people wondered and wondered and wondered, and as if no people whispered and said it could not possibly have been him, the facts didn't fit. The neighbour who spoke to Maud, years later, said that nobody believed this was going to stick.

"We neither believed that he did it nor that the case would be continued. We were a bit shocked to find that it was going to a court in Dublin, but we thought that, traumatic as this might be, everything would turn out all right in the end and Harry would be back here soon."

They also had ideas as to who might have been involved. Moll Graney's life had caused many anxieties in her local community, none more active than those of the fathers of some of her children. And there were visitors to her house who would prefer never to be known. Indeed, among them was a guard in the station where Harry Tavey was brought to be questioned. And to complete local frisson, Moll worked occasionally in the garda station.

"I have great crack altogether down at the guards," she said often.

There were a lot of people who would not have wished Moll Graney to say a lot of things. Harry Tavey was not one of those. And worse than that, there were growing children, whose resemblance to local men was becoming startlingly apparent as they became older. She lived a dangerous life, this woman alone, feeding her children. A dangerous life and a dangerous death.

When the Mountjoy Prison door closed on Harry Tavey, he tried to think of tunes. He tried to think of weather. He tried to think of farm work. But the only thing that would stay in his mind was the door and the sound of the lock hitting into place. And yet, as he sat on the bed to think his way through the next few months, he did believe that nothing of any real harm would come to him. He did believe that a man cannot be found guilty of something he did not do. He did believe that he would soon be back home.

The questioning of neighbours continued. Those who said the things that made it impossible for Harry Tavey to have committed this murder were left aside. Those who suggested otherwise, by innuendo and overenthusiastic agreement with what they thought the questions meant, were taken seriously. Those who had no reason to like outsiders were believed more than those who saw the man, who played tunes with him, who played hurling with him, who walked with him, who had an occasional stout with him, who talked with him. The gathering of these comments was like a hurricane happening behind Harry's back, who, while he sat in Mountjoy, was completely unaware of the storm taking shape. And even worse was to happen.

Two guards visited the hardware store in Cashel, where most of the ammunition used in the New Inn area was purchased. They inspected the firearms register and pointed out to staff that it contained no record of any sale to Harry Tavey's uncle, on the date that they mentioned, of cartridges of a type that they also mentioned. They suggested that on their next visit they would see such an entry. And Maud saw the entry. She stared at it disbelievingly. The clear crossing out of another man's name, not even erased to the extent that she could not read it. Above it was scrawled exactly the information that the guards had given to the staff in the hardware store. This any person can see to this day.

The black winds edged closer and closer together. Men who had heard one shot, two shots, at times when Harry Tavey could not have been in that area were not believed or had their minds changed or had doubts kneaded into them. Men who could not, because of the direction of the wind on the day, have heard any shots from the spots on which they were standing had now suddenly heard an exact lucid sound. This is the place where certainty is no longer certain. If Harry Tavey had not moved quite happily into the first reel on that night, if Harry Tavey had drawn breath when he arrived in the house of the dance, if Harry Tavey had turned his head around and said to the next man, "I thought I heard shots tonight, just when I was passing Reilly's hedge. Who would be out shooting at that hour of the night? Sure, you could see nothing." If Harry Tavey had said that, to any one man, then things might have been different.

So he thought, as he sat in his cell. Then he thought so many things, so many things that could prove that he did not do this, and yet there was no one in this place to hear them.

In good moments, when he had shaken himself up and told himself to get through this strong, he knew that his neighbours would be fine. He knew that they would piece another story together. And it was this knowing that held the saddest truth of all. It was this knowing that sent shivers up Maud's spine as she tried to go to sleep at night.

As Harry Tavey sat on his bed, lay on his bed, walked in his small cell, an uncontrollable story was growing outside, an edifice of lies was maturing into fact. *And it remains to this day*, Maud thought.

At the court in Green Street, Harry's aunt and uncle, cousin, and a few friends huddled together, as if caught in a snow storm of half-truths that fell from the mouths of those who gave evidence. As his defence chipped and chipped at what they knew to be untrue, the friends sometimes galvanised themselves with the consolation that was creeping into their bad dreams. But they knew little of the law. They knew little of the place they were staying. They had never stayed in a bed and breakfast in the centre of Dublin before this. The food in cafés near by was strange. Harry's aunt's varicose veins were playing up. But they could tell what wasn't true, and in their innocence believed that so, too, could the jury. But that was not what happened on those days, in that place, at that time. The jury believed what the others said. Harry Tavey was found guilty of a murder that he did not commit. His aunt and uncle had delayed over the last cup of tea at lunchtime and were coming up the street when two neighbours approached them. They seemed to be walking on the sides of their feet and were ashen faced. The wails of Harry's aunt may still be heard on the corner of Green Street if a person listens closely.

Harry was put into a van and brought back to Mountjoy.

"But it isn't true," he repeated to himself, as if the words could save him. Harry moved into his cell and again worked on himself to believe that an appeal would succeed. But the appeal did not succeed either. In the days that followed the appeal failure, guards from outside the locality still visited the scene, still asked questions, still wondered about odd pieces of evidence that clashed completely with other sworn statements. They had great questions; they felt in their bones that a wrong verdict had been created. But the neighbours closed their doors to new questions. They wanted this horror gone from them. They wanted someone to be blamed. They wanted to put that night, that morning, these weeks, behind them. They wanted never to speak of it again. And it was easier; a person from outside the neighbourhood was always a better bet than one of their own. Those who knew he was innocent then travelled to Dublin to meet the minister for justice. But it was too late. The die was cast and the outcome was already written. Harry Tavey prepared for his own unjust death.

* * *

Although Maud pored over the huge question that lay across the spoken words of those who gave evidence, she knew that nothing could change the exact sequence of events. Although she could see with absolute clarity exactly what was right and what was wrong, there was no way to make this thing not have happened. She became lonely in a ferocious kind of way.

CHAPTER 16

MAUD WENT ON a hospital visit to see Bernie from the office. Bernie was having some tests, a new concept in their workplace, the first person among Maud's age group to be mysterious about an ailment, which must mean that she was seriously worried. There was an air of disbelief among her colleagues. That any one of them could actually get ill was a ridiculous thought. Maud didn't like visiting her but felt obliged. The smell jolted her back to that other evening, but she made herself think of something else, because she had become an expert at superseding memory so that she didn't suddenly stand still, in inappropriate places, rooted to the spot with grief. She even now tried to tell herself that her parents had had a good innings, which was ludicrous; they had only been in their fifties. That her mother might have liked to have got old, with photographs stacking up on the shelves, the faces of her children changing into structures, faint lines gathering speed at family functions, may have been true, but how could one possibly bear to think about that?

The corridor was busy. Friends and relatives stood outside some rooms. Expectant, and oblivious of passers-by, they whispered, the sounds muffled as if the whole show was under water. By the time Maud reached Bernie's ward, the patient was up, dressed and putting her few belongings into the overnight bag. Everything was fine; it had been a false alarm.

"See, I told you. Great."

Of course, they were too young. Maud left Bernie, who was waiting for her lift home, already departed from this room of panic. Maud took a short cut out the back of the hospital wings. A young doctor with two inches of black underneath his eyes was stealing a cigarette. He jumped as if caught fornicating in the open.

"Next time I'm sick I hope I get you. And I hope I can smell it off you."

The doctor laughed in relief or shame. From where did that bit of flirting fly out? Maud was pleased with herself. There could be another life. Now, was there anyone she could telephone? Some woman with whom to go on a skite.

* * *

She hadn't intended to have no one close friend, but her best school friend, Patricia, lived in San Francisco. Her next best friend, Julia, had publicly snubbed her one evening in a bar for the sake of more interesting company. And things were never quite the same between them since. But in truth she hadn't missed Julia's company all that much. She talked enough at work, had an adequate social life with friendships that skimmed the surfaces of intimacy. And there was always Malachy. Alone or with Valerie. But what, when all this was over, if she really needed a woman to be there? Would she be able to get that independent dependency going with someone now? Or would she have left it too late? Because that state did require a certain amount of absolute loyalty, borne only from shared history. She knew this now because she was tempted to telephone Patricia and tell her the lot. But it wasn't strictly true that it was the ocean which caused the separation between Maud and Patricia. It was time, and diverging interests, and now the fear that Patricia might already have been told, that the whole friendship might have been based on a pity of sorts. Still, this couldn't be true. Patricia had begged her to come with her for the summer job, their last year at secondary school.

The job was in Dublin. It would be preparation for city living: six weeks, wardsmaid, chambermaid in doctor's residence, general dogsbody for whatever needed doing in a hospital near the Green, private patients to be served first, among them a famous singer. Live-in across the lane. It was here that Maud discovered that everyone was not interested in the same things. Certainly not in most of the things that took up her ruminating time, the hide and seek thoughts, the scraps waiting for mental order to be put upon them. You could possibly find one thing that interested everybody. Perhaps the idea that the day would start later? But even that couldn't be guaranteed, because there would always be some loop-the-loo who liked early mornings, some farmer's daughter who had got up every morning to help around the byre before going to school, who liked the fact that she had a weather check done before the weather men were up.

Patricia knew how to have conversations with everybody. One minute it was whether or not to keep up Latin at university (this was with a Louis girl, of course), the next it was the merits of domestic science versus art (a Mercy girl). Waitressing or bar work. Places to go, fashion, fabrics, make-up, the difficulties of getting eyeliner straight, the best way to handle boys, the looks of boys and religion; religion, for Christ's sake. Maud stayed as close to her slipstream as possible. The morning of the fight, she ran into Patricia's cubicle and got into her bed.

Sister Ministris called a new girl for the third time. The parish priest had got the girl the job. Still lying in bed, she pulled back the curtains and growled, "Don't you call me again."

The nerve of it lifted the hearts of twenty-four listening girls. But some fool, there's always one, chirped, "I don't think you should speak to Sister like that. She's only doing her job."

There was a quick ripping back of curtains, a sound that could almost have been a slap, but that couldn't be possible. A few seconds stunned silence and then a squeal of shock and pain. What a terrible thing for that new girl to do. But more surprisingly, Sister Ministris' ally rushed into the cubicle and slapped back. The new girl punched her in the face like a man would. The ally hit again. Other girls screamed. Some were clearly frightened and one cried, "Mammy." One more slap, another, then the two laid aside the rules that were never meant for them anyway. They clawed, scratched and pulled hair on their way to the sack. By the time the fight was stopped, Maud was in Patricia's bed shaking with terror,

Patricia was trying to see as much of the fight as she possibly could while holding and shushing Maud.

Both fighters were marched to the back door. So much for being an ally. One step out and the bat on the mouth is yours as surely as the instigator's. Sister Ministris was relieved from morning call duty for ever. Although routines were recovered, they did not quite have their accustomed assurance, and wouldn't until the last of the girls who had seen the action had departed from these cubicles. Yet, shocking and all as the behaviour of that morning was, the unpredictability of it made the girls more interested in their own sex.

Maud wasn't sure. On the night of their first late-night pass, she went to a dance, with Patricia, of course. It was the strangest thing, to know the music and yet to recognise not one face. Maud checked her watch continuously to see when this would be over. At home she would have resented the thought of the last dance. Patricia enjoyed herself. Thank God, she didn't meet a man. Maud wouldn't have known how to play gooseberry in a city; no doubt the rules were different. As they neared their dormitory, they heard the rattle of the trolley used to remove the dead to the morgue, Tin Lizzy, the Box; it sent the shivers up Maud's spine. They rounded the corner of the morgue, Patricia oblivious, Maud pretending the same. And then she was hit on the face with a wet dish cloth. She didn't squeal, she wailed. The perpetrator hopped on Tin Lizzy and was wheeled noisily away, hooting laughter into the sky. Maud gave up all pretence of bravery and moved into Patricia's bed permanently. No, it couldn't be true that a mere ocean and eight hours time difference could have caused a separation in such a friendship. Maybe she would talk to Patricia. After Malachy.

CHAPTER 17

WHEN HARRY ASKED to talk to Leo Boland, the prison officer, Leo thought, *Oh, God, here we go again. This is the start of it. What have I done to deserve this?* A condemned man could take a liking to an officer. He could sense who was trustworthy, who might be able to stand in the small cell without making it smaller, who might be able to play cards quietly on night watch, who might be able to understand yearnings for the little privacies of man without having to be told. In his navy uniform with the high collar, his buttons shining a dance when hit by the sun, his shoes blue-black with gloss, all accentuating his massive good looks, Leo got noticed by condemned men. And then they would plead with him to accompany them to their hangings. Him, who had a wife to go home to, to sleep with. And children.

Not only a wife and children, but one who still looked at him when he came home in the evenings. It often took him by surprise. And this work had seemed a good idea at the time: steady money, inside work, no street walking. His wife told him not to turn the job about in his mind too much. She said it would be bad for him. She said that all he had to do was treat the prisoners right, as if they were human beings like themselves, which they were, as if there but for the grace of God. . . And he did whatever she told him to do about those kind of matters because she knew best. Normally. But he wondered if treating the men well didn't reap its own disadvantages.

This was the third condemned man who had taken a liking to him. The bullies who had become thicker with every wage packet, who had grown fists in their hearts, were never requested by a prisoner. They might be sent all right, by the governor, but they were never requested. And this new man would want him to come to the hanging. He was shaping up to it. Leo could tell better than the man himself; he'd been here before. The man would need one face there who could watch the parting of his body from his soul and know that it was wrong. That it was hard. That he was terrified. That he wanted to cry. But the prisoner, this Harry fellow, wouldn't think about how he, Leo, would have to live with this for ever. Couldn't they just send two priests? Wasn't that supposed to be their job? Of course, the last one hadn't looked at the prisoner at all, probably ashamed of himself, probably ordered there by the bishop, although they're supposed to know that this is not right. And here they would all be, upholders of the law, a doctor and a priest, all together at a hanging. It made no sense to Leo.

Leo's wife could tell him to try to banish it out of his mind, it was all right for her. She only had a name for the man, no face, no looks, no sound of him. His wife didn't wish him to be a harsh man, nor a big thick ignorant gulpin if you want to put it another way, but that is the only thing that could save him. To become a big thick ignorant gulpin. Yet he hadn't got the material inside himself to do that, so instead he did his best to see through each day, as if there was a heaven on the other side of it.

Harry was a good card player. He sometimes hummed tunes absentmindedly when he turned in for the night. It didn't seem as if he heard the tunes himself, more that they had just come out with his breath. He sighed a lot in his sleep, and one night whimpered like either a dog or a child. Leo hated sitting awake watching, guarding, hearing gusts of the lonely sleeping dreams of a condemned man. Under the skin of those dreams, Harry was a free man and none of this had happened. Still, Leo would have to brace himself and do his job. The last officer who had refused to go to the edge of the trap door with a prisoner was given a dog's life until the day he quit the job. After that he had visited the dark corners of various pubs, drinking his family into hunger. There was too much time for Leo to think, while the other officer snored and Harry shot sleeping yelps of despair into the long dark minutes of the night.

Leo was given the job of telling Harry about the failure of his appeal. Harry's eyes blanked out for a few seconds and then moistened.

"I thought as much," he said.

He wrung his hands and paced the room. Then he laughed an eerie sound.

"I'm like a caged greyhound. You know I didn't do it, but that hardly matters. The sooner now the better, don't you think, Leo? Do you mind if I call you Leo?"

"No, not at all, not at all."

"Yes, the sooner now the better. I could never have gone back there anyway, not after all this. Yes, the sooner now the better."

It was almost a relief to get to the last morning. The bustling terror was pressed down with rituals stacked back to back. A last visit, the shaving of the man, the priest's prayers, swallowing to wet a dry mouth. Leo shook Harry's hand, all the time staring at the wall opposite him. He had intended to look the man in the eye but lost his nerve at the last minute. He walked behind him, down the corridor, up the steps, stood solidly beside the prisoner. After the blindfolding and just before the door was opened, he stretched out his hand, letting it rest momentarily on the prisoner's shoulder. That might make up for his eyes having been fixed on the wall.

"Harry, it's me, Leo. God be good to you."

"Right, Leo, thanks for all you've done for me."

Oh God, he is thanking me. Don't thank, please, please, please don't thank me.

The noise swung the last second of Harry's life into oblivion.

After that day, Leo took a week off sick, during which time he made love to his wife in a way that we don't think was commonly done at the time.

CHAPTER 18

THREE LETTERS HAD come and gone between Maud and Xavier before he was given his date. Maud was guiltily grateful that the smallness of the number put her outside the immediate panic. Xavier did send her a postcard, announcing his date, as one would a wedding or a get-together or a birth. He asked her to pray for him on the following Thursday week at the appointed hour. He had worked out the time difference. She didn't know where to hide the card, carried it around like a precious but dangerous thing, putting it behind pictures, under the mattress, then finally tucking it in at the bottom of her mother's sewing box. It would be fine there. Care had been taken of it. Perhaps that care would change minds.

There was no mention of the pending execution in the Irish newspapers. There wasn't enough about it that made it significantly different from any other. Maud slept in spasms the night before. She had to command herself not to think of the preparations. It was the preparations that got to her most. She put the morning in at work in a listless way. People remarked how pale she was. As the hour approached, she feigned an illness to match the pallor. She wanted to be outside when the time came. Out in a place where she could swing her arms. As she walked down the street, she felt her heart drop for a second, as if it had actually, momentarily, fallen from its place. "Oh dear," she said out loud. She went home, telephoned Amnesty International to check that it really had been done. They said sorry, yes. And it had been at the time she knew. A month later, a cousin of Xavier's sent her a thank you note and a memorial card.

CHAPTER 19

ND SO, AMERICA called Maud again, like an unreasonable invitation handed out in a dream. This was going to be difficult. She was going to go further into the nether jaws this time. And she was still going to do it in secrecy, she decided. If she told Malachy he might stop her, not by order or plea but by the sense of his displeasure. She had silent conversations with him, sometimes while on the verge of sleeping or waking. They were walking away from each other in that comfortable manner that they always used, but while he was preparing to turn back, was getting ready to smile at their perfect symmetry, she was marching straight on, getting further and further away, lips creased into a hardened jaw, eyes scrunched up as if there was sun in her face. His disappointment, almost growing into fury, filled her bedroom. Secrecy it would have to be. And then there was work.

Maud began at the last point of her previous journey. She bought a side table where she strewed contact numbers, pieces of paper with plans. She opted for flexi-time in her job so that she could make telephone calls from home during the office hours of others.

"Good morning, Aer Lingus booking office."

"Good morning. Could you tell me the price of your return tickets to America?"

A voice listed the options.

"OK. I'll be back to you."

She worked up time off so she could telephone America during its waking hours.

"Good morning, Amnesty International. How can I help you?"

"I want to do two things: I want to visit a death row and I want to meet those Journey whatever-you-call-them. You told me about them the last time I was there."

That was pretty succinct.

"Oh yes. The Journey of Hope people. Actually it's called 'The Journey of Hope from Violence to Healing'. I think there are two groups, so one needs to be specific."

"Well, Journeyers will do for the purposes of this call, otherwise I'll be on the phone all day," Maud said, an almost cheery inflection in her voice. Action was a bracing thing.

"Yes," the man said, resigned to the fact that different countries had different senses of humour. In order to get it right, or rather not wrong, one had to sedate one's voice with blandness. "Once a year, family members of murder victims who do not agree with capital punishment converge in a particular state. They visit schools, colleges, churches. They speak about their personal experiences and explain their position."

Oh yes, Xavier had told her about those people.

"There will also be relatives of death row inmates on the journey. They, too, will speak. It's Tennessee this year. Can I have your address and I'll send you the information. I'll also send you our updated list of death row inmates and a list of each of the prisons."

"Fine, fine."

Maud spelled her address. Tennessee might be nice. They had rolling hills, didn't they? What were the cities? She would deal with her nervousness by concentrating on geography. Yes, rolling hills, Nashville, country music, Chattanooga Choo-Choo, Memphis, Tennessee. Long straight roads, wind in her hair; no, there would be no roll-top Greyhound buses. The map was the next thing. She examined the atlas with all the concentration of a concerned tourist. She could have been a tour organiser searching for the definitive route, a serious woman looking for an obscure place of importance, a surface traveller looking for famous city names to notch on her belt. What Maud needed was a plan. Visit prison first, then meet those traveller people. But which prison? And why would she pick one over another? Should she go to the one in the top of the league for worst reputation or one less scourging? Should she fly straight to Nashville, visit their one and then hook up with those people?

But Maud decided that she would like to see New York again. And a little of the countryside. She would also like a few days alone, before the visit, before meeting those people, who might be strange. Watertight change of flight insurance on her ticket would be essential, in case she lost her nerve. So she opened the New York and Environs page, closed her eyes against the light, and wandered her fingers over the page. She would choose the nearest to where her finger stopped. Around and around, slow down, there. There. The tip of her finger was to the west of Philadelphia. Which translated into Graterford Prison. She was one step nearer to the plan.

* * *

Maud spent the following weeks securing permission to visit death row. And decided to call it, simply, the prison. It seemed less threatening. There were letters of reference to be acquired. The priest at home would do that. The guards would have to be asked. She would organise all that from her parents' town, which she still called home. It would be easier there, less likely to land back on a desk at her work. The locals would not need to ask questions; she had been known since she was a child. She would say that she was applying for a visa, thinking of a long stay abroad. Now she would have to find out which countries required such stringent vetting. This sub-terfuge was hard work. It required the amassing of knowledge that she would not be able to use elsewhere. Still, the business attached to the preparation stopped her thinking about what she was really doing. It might have been, most certainly would have been, easier to tell someone. If not Malachy, one of her friends, even a distant acquaintance who could be sworn to secrecy. But it crossed Maud's mind only fleetingly. She knew the dangers of prattling, saw them daily, as a shared confi-dence was shredded, gnawed over and elevated to public gos-sip. A loud whisper with a sting in it. What fodder she could give them.

It was time for a night out, because these would soon have to be limited. She would have to be careful with her money, the Aer Lingus section of the cost the only one remaining static. Telephone calls were mounting up. Greyhound bus prices were cheaper than she had expected, but Amtrak trains were much dearer, and there would be hotels. She regularly crossed off numbers that had been dead ends. Regularly made new lists. Gerard's New York number seemed to get bigger each time she wrote it out, but it remained unrung. Her telephone calls regarding permission to visit had to be played right. She became an expert at the art of overhearing nuances, even in unfamiliar accents.

The guards and priest at home were delighted to see her. They couldn't reference her up high enough. They asked about Malachy. They wondered to each other if Maud was as well as she seemed, slightly nervous, the guard thought. He was given to being sympathetic when in doubt, long ago having come to the conclusion that there was a great amount of good in the worst of us. The priest's view was more pinched, long ago having come to the conclusion that there could be a great amount of bad in the best of us. He wondered if Maud wasn't running away too soon; running away never solved anything. Why, if you were faced with a mountain lion, the experts told you not to run, to face it, to make yourself bigger than you were. But then, as always, he deflated from his high horse because his faith had trained him that the guard was probably right. At Maud's local Dublin post office, the old counter-hand, who looked annoyingly like her mother, sensed the importance of these letters. She was long enough at her job to read the way stamps were stuck on envelopes.

"If you post on Tuesday, it's better for America, I've always thought," she remarked.

"That was before aeroplanes," Maud answered, with an uncharacteristic dose of putdown in her voice. The woman decided to ignore it because she had to. Maud was getting jumpy. She was riveted by the secrecy of her plans but made nervous by them, too. She hadn't known the depth of her own determination. She longed to talk to Malachy, mostly because she couldn't. It was definitely time for the night out.

* * *

She made arrangements with Majorie and Caitríona, the co-workers with whom she dreamed of holidaying, and Malachy and Valerie. She bought a skin-coloured bra that had transparent cups. The garment begged for an audience. They went to hear a band in Whelan's bar. Maud had a new relationship with fiddle players. Where once, in her ignorance, she had heard a discordant tone veering dangerously towards a screech, now she heard a full colour running. The crowd was enjoying itself; the band was enjoying the crowd enjoying itself.

"You're going on holidays to America again? What are you not telling us?" Valerie asked.

"It's a poor family that cannot afford one gentleman, and she's ours," Malachy said defensively.

And one liar, Valerie thought.

The music stayed loud enough to cover any discomfort. There was always a sharpness between Maud and Valerie. Maud thought about it. Not jealousy: she was happy that Malachy was happy. It was just that she had expected him to get someone more thoughtful, more capable of listening, someone who could let a sentence be finished before jumping in with her ludicrous comparisons. Oh dear, it was time to make an effort. Because when she did, these things could be smoothed over. The ball was in her court, seemed to land back there every time. Valerie didn't think about it. Malachy did, and always told himself that it was caused by possessiveness. He knew that this was not the whole truth, but it was the only one which was bearable.

Maud suggested that they go to South Street; the food was cheap enough, and the house red was great.

"Are the girls from the office coming?" Valerie asked.

Maud bristled. The girls from the office were women with highly responsible jobs. Still, keep trying, keep trying. And the girls from the office did come, kicking up their legs on their way down the street. The food was fine, the wine perfect, Caitríona told jokes, Malachy and Valerie sign-languaged to each other, and Maud felt afraid of her secret. They split the bill, slipped into their coats and straggled out.

Caitríona said, "Let's go to Reynard's."

"Not us, not us," Valerie said, so fast it almost came out on top of Caitríona's words.

"Why not?" said Maud and Majorie, both of them having been relieved that someone else wanted more drink and afraid that one defection might threaten the possibility.

They kissed and hugged Valerie and Malachy, who turned away to get a taxi. Maud felt sorry for him, remembering when he had tried to spin out the minutes until dawn, when he had tried not to let people go to bed. Malachy felt sorry for Maud, going off to a nightclub crush. But he turned back when they were a few yards away. He waved at his sister, twitching an umbilical cord between them, and felt better for it.

At the club they talked nonsense until it came out their ears. They got giddy on the frivolity and the bad wine. Caitríona launched into confidences with glittering suddenness.

"You must know Caitríona Le Fanu, she's from your county?" Caitríona said.

Majorie said, "What an odd combination of names."

Maud straightened her glass. Caitríona said, "Yes, that Caitríona. She named herself after me when she had the sex change done. It's a bit embarrassing. It's not like having a niece called after you."

Keep talking, Maud thought. *Keep going, until I get time to come up with an appropriate response.*

"We don't talk about it much in our family, as you can imagine. He was my father's brother before; now I suppose he's my father's sister. She."

That's long enough, Maud thought. *I should have something to say now.*

"Yes, I can imagine."

The inadequacy of her reply might sound flippant or, worse still, judgemental. She was trying for something else. Hard to say what was the best tone to strike. Surely she could do better. But how? Does one sympathise? Crack a joke? To behave as if this were normal might be insulting.

"What do you mean?" said Majorie, her mouth remaining open at the end of the question, which was a good thing, because it allowed Maud to explain factually without trimmings what she now remembered reading in the newspaper about Caitríona's relation. Caitríona seemed relieved.

"Would you like to dance, ladies?" said three voices of men suddenly positioned at each of their shoulders.

"Later," came the choral lying reply, as each of them turned to gratefully accept the offer. In the dance they tried to work off the embarrassment of Caitríona's confidence. Maud refused the second dance,

"I really do mean that I will dance later, in a few moments. There's something I need to finish first."

Caitríona also refused her dance. Majorie stayed on the floor. One sensed she would have stayed with the man even if he had cloven feet, anything rather than go back to their corner at the bar. Double yellow lines had been painted over it. Maud and Caitríona slid on to their seats.

"I sometimes talk about it; I suppose I shouldn't. I forget that other people might not understand," Caitríona said.

"I do. Believe me, I do," said Maud.

Here was her opportunity; now was the time; they would both benefit. But Maud let the chance slip uncontrollably away from her. And Caitríona explained about all the unhappiness of her Uncle Charles and all the shock, and then how blood proved itself to be so much thicker than water it took her breath away.

"Even my father," she said.

"Well, that's good," Maud said, wondering if calamity had degrees, or if one simply eventually embraced one's own so tight that it melted into the natural sequence of one's history. She looked around as unobtrusively as possible, hoping to send a signal to her dancer. She saw him on the floor deeply engrossed with a woman who was obviously not going to drop him after one dance, a woman who had nothing more serious to attend to than her and his needs. Ah well, her new bra could do without being seen.

Majorie stayed with her man. The four of them shared a taxi home. Majorie said, with indecent haste, "We'll drop Caitríona off first." Maud could have argued that her flat was closest, but Caitríona said, "Great," as if she meant it.

At home Maud threw her smokey clothes around the room, repeating, "Phew," with an understandable measure of *schadenfreude*. In the morning she woke, her mouth filled with one big Phew.

* * *

Malachy dropped in the following Saturday morning. The grace of God, and some minor emergency of Valerie's, took him away before the telephone rang. It was Chief Superintendent Donald J. Calvin, of Graterford Department of Corrections, State Correctional Institution at Graterford.

"How is the weather in Ireland? I've never been there myself. Meant to drop in one time we were in Europe. Had a friend who stopped over in Shannon. I suppose that doesn't count."

"Hello, hello, yes. No. Well, yes, yes."

Maud shifted from one foot to the other, thinking that she would have to come up with something longer than one-syllable words. She was frightened. She had allowed the voice of a man who worked "there" for a living into her home. Not just allowed, invited. The telephone caused a vague numbness in her arm, the sort that followed the first cigarette of the day. A cigarette, yes, that might do it. She lit up and dragged in.

"Oh yes, it's a chilly day." What comes next?

"Chilly, chilly. I like when you say chilly."

They could have been old mates.

"Chilly but bright."

Was she saying chilly because Chief Superintendent Donald J. Calvin liked it or was the needle stuck? *Pretend you're at work.*

"So. Is everything in order?"

"Yes, no problem. You have been approved. A letter of permission will arrive with instructions about how you must conduct the visit. So we will see you then. Ireland, nice place, I believe. My wife and I do intend to make it some day. Or have I told you that before? Goodbye, goodbye."

The phone was dead.

"Goodbye," said Maud.

She could still step back, ignore the letter. This was going too near the past. And how far removed was this from her granduncle? She would telephone or write to cancel, because she had manners.

CHAPTER 20

MAUD NEVER DID telephone to cancel. She hid the letter in the sewing box. She pinpointed the area and had maps blown up. She tried in vain to find out how she could get there. She telephoned the prison three times, fortifying herself with a small Cinzano and tonic and as many cigarettes as it took. Each time the instructions were different, leading her in contradictory directions according to her blown-up map. She began to sleep in instalments, bobbing up slightly, then falling asleep again when she realised that the day of departure was not actually upon her yet. Anxiety came in wafts like whipped-up wind. It was easier to get up too early. She got annoyed with people over the simplest of things, snapped at people at work, blew up with Valerie, risked all the equilibriums she had established in her life.

"Maud really does need a holiday," said Valerie, using far more diplomacy than was expected of her, notching up brownie points to beat the band. She even organised a lunch before Maud left, showing a skill with avocado and orange salad, gazpacho and a variety of cheeses that couldn't leave anyone disappointed. She invited the girls from the office. Majorie gave Caitríona a lift. People can get used to anything. Maud wanted to talk to Malachy. No, not yet. As soon as she got home. It was only for twelve days.

She packed, putting photocopies of the letter in as many different places as she could find, and in all three small bags. All of them could not go missing. If she lost her handbag, she would not be carrying the others. Neuroticism might not be far away. She managed to avoid the Malachy and Valerie caravan to the airport, getting a taxi instead. Valerie had given her the gift of Valium. She seemed to have a supply at the ready, without embarrassment. The tablet soothed her stomach and stopped the rushes of adrenalin that threatened to end in tears. During turbulence, Maud clutched the armrests, the ashtrays mocking her.

"You'd think they'd remove them, wouldn't you?" the man next to her said. "Now that they allow smoking nowhere," he added.

As the plane prepared to land, she changed her watch to New York time. The couple on the other side of her didn't. They were returning to work in New York and wished to keep their watches on home time for as long as possible.

Articles of the Bill of Rights were artistically proclaimed along the corridor. She hadn't seen them on her first visit. Maybe she had exited by a different route. Cerulean blue on

Paynes grey, straight lines, clear letters, above the moving side-walk. Article VIII: "Excessive bail shall not be required, nor excessive fines imposed, nor cruel and unusual punishment inflicted."

Maud was surprised at this artwork. She probably wouldn't have noticed it if her mind had not been engaged as it was. She read it again. Problem solved. Maybe she should tell someone. At the baggage collection point, people who had talked non-stop during the flight had already blown fully into New York mode. They were now silent and busy. Her bag welcomed her to claim it.

At the ground transportation desk, there was a switch back to effusive helpfulness. This time Maud knew to keep her wits about her in order to follow the right leads. She could not start any of her own, would have to respond, not initiate. And she would concentrate on small things and on the smells of glori-ous coffees to avoid the real reason for her visit. She would have to wait a half an hour for the Greylink transport. She ran to the telephone, clutching Gerard's telephone number. One half hour and she couldn't bear it. He was delighted to hear her voice, may have been taken aback, but Maud selfishly wanted him to drop everything to meet her for a drink after she got to her hotel. He would. He might have to tell lies — who knew? Maud didn't care.

"Philadelphia and Tennessee on holidays? My what a little traveller. I'll meet you, Time Café, 7.30. Would that be OK?"

Two glasses of dry white wine roved in on the tail-end of Valerie's Valium and she was all his. They went to her bedroom where she stretched along him. He had to leave soon after-wards, but that was OK with Maud. She knew that he was puzzled, would have liked better explanations, maybe deserved them. Before he left, she drew the top sheet around her and said, "I will tell you about my holiday next time. By the way, how would I find out the easiest way to get to Graterford, Philadelphia? I have an aunt there, but I can't seem to find the best way."

Gerard got on the phone, yessed and yessed and yessed, and then handed her a piece of paper with the easiest route carefully marked on it, kissed her on the mouth and closed the door quietly.

* * *

In order to alleviate her panic, Maud practised self-satisfaction on the way to Port Authority. The Greyhound bus bound for King of Prussia glided past swirls of trade names. If only they meant something to her. If only they reminded her of something. She finally got directions to the car hire office after she had cleared her throat a number of times. The first time her voice came out squeaky; the second time the office clerk could not understand her. Having rented the car, she dared to ask directions to Graterford. And where the nearest hotel might be.

"I know someone out that way. Hold on a moment, I'll call."

He handed her a piece of paper and explained. The 2025 as far as 422 West to Exit 26B, Collegeville, to 29 North for five miles.

"Thank you, thank you very much."

Maud fiddled with the automatic trappings as a farmer might examine a borrowed plough. She couldn't very well return to ask how to use it; the hirer might think it best to retrieve the property. She drove too carefully up the road, conscious that there was a bulk of car to her right hand, and that she must at all times remain on her correct side of the road. She was glad of the slow speed limit and used it fully, to the annoyance of drivers behind her, she was sure.

"The tax will have run out on this car by the time you get around that roundabout," Malachy had said when she took him for his first drive in her new car. Maud smiled and picked up a little speed. Exit 26B. The road got narrower. It was important to hug the middle line; it was important not to miss the next turn. The bends rode into one another. The line of cars behind her grew longer; their collective patience was admirable. Where could she possibly pull over? There. But where were the indicators? Damn, there was the Graterford Hotel. There was no place to pull over. Surely the patience behind her would explode. Five miles further on she pulled into a gas station — how quickly one loses allegiance to one's own words. Now this would be the test, she would enquire straight out how to get to the prison. She wanted to have it located so that there would be no hiccups in the morning. The man she asked was nonchalant. There had been no need to worry.

"Back that way. Take a left over the bridge, at the Graterford Hotel."

And so she did. Out into the real country, through hedgeless fields, winding away further from the town, past the warning signs, the dos and don'ts of prison approach, closer to the walls. There was the car park. Now she would get out of here fast. Find a bed.

A woman was hitching a lift. There was no public transport to here; life would not be made easy for family or friends.
As Maud turned the car — where the hell was reverse? — she
wondered if she should take the woman as passenger, but was
relieved to see a uniformed man stop to offer a lift. The
woman would have to swallow any pride still left. What would
her poor man inside think if he could see her? Presumably this
woman was visiting an ordinary prisoner. Maud believed that
the demeanour of those visiting the other kind would be such
as to mark them out like beacons.

She wound her way back out and tried to find, from
among the litter of signs, one for a hotel. She decided against
the Graterford; she needed somewhere larger, more anony-
mous. The next two queries proved fruitless. One had no
room. Maud raised her eyebrows sarcastically to herself. No
one she knew would want her to stay there anyway. The other
was closed for renovation. Maud didn't believe them. She was
getting tired and hungry. And then in Pottstown, like manna,
there it was: the Holiday Inn, an American version of the Ibis,
a version of an Irish B&B, the stable, the relief of worried travellers. There would be a bed there, and there was, no question.
Twelfth floor, smoking room, coffee machine, restaurant
through the car park. Maud's throat was sore, and an aeroplane
sinus came late, pressing on her head like dead weight.

After food she went gratefully to her room and longed to be
able to make telephone calls. But the strenuous telling of lies at
this point would require too much effort. She emptied her bag.
The strings of notes that had got her here, the log of pointless
and useful calls, were all now on the floor. On her way to the
bathroom for a power driven shower, she glanced at them as if

they were the sediments of someone else's plan, surely not hers. What had this got to do with her? Whatever could have brought her to this town, this room, alone? Alone, and embarked for the seeing of a sight that might keep her awake for ever. Perhaps it would not be so bad. Take back the bed covers of a bed as big as her room at home, take consolation from warmth that is as familiar as breathing, go to sleep. And Maud did sleep.

She was bathed, dressed, and made up before the wake-up call clanged into her room. She had woken out of a fully fledged discussion with an unknown voice.

"Have you ever thought of what some of these men have done? Oh no, bet you haven't. Bleeding heart liberal. Fry them all."

"Would you do it yourself?"

"No problem. Pull the switch."

"Do you know that it's not over just like that?"

"Who cares? Look what they did."

"Some of them didn't. So if one is killed wrongly, you, who care so much about wrongful killing, who then must die for that? The executioner, the judge, the lawyers, the jury perhaps?"

"It doesn't happen often."

"Is not often enough?"

"Oh, yeah."

There goes Harry, her uncle, Granduncle Harry. Funny, he had receded from her mind since getting on the plane, but he was with her this morning. She had woken abruptly, catapulted into wakefulness, and Harry was in the room with her as surely as if she had known him all her life, as surely as if she knew him still. He would be with her all day.

Maud went to breakfast in the lobby, remembering to take

her bag with her. She ate, drank lukewarm tea and, mindful of her money and the larger question of waste, rolled bread and fruit into her bag for later eating, as a sixties hippie might have done. She booked out, playing the part of an ordinary traveller well, or so she thought.

"Which road do I take to Collegeville?"

She knew, but she needed something for conversation. The receptionist began to give directions. The cleaner butted in.

"And after Collegeville, you don't have to turn until you come to Graterford. The prison is up to the right."

The receptionist frowned at the intrusion. Maud thought, *Oh shit, that obvious?*

"And after Collegeville comes?" That would teach her to make assumptions.

"Graterford," said the receptionist, trapped in the picture that had been flashed up by the cleaner.

"Thank you," said Maud, mustering up a body language that would get her out of here and into that car.

It was a heavy misty day. She recognised flashes of the road. She concentrated on her driving, picking up a little speed, engaging herself in normal thoughts. *My! My! what wonderful houses, here is the bridge, my what a long road up, here is the sign, look at that bird, well here's the car park.* She got out of the car quickly and made her way to the front entrance.

At the desk she passed over the often-checked letter. As the woman glanced over it, Maud flicked some fluff off her jacket. She was glad she had ironed her shirt. She would have been just as glad if she hadn't. A baby cried in the background; it was a steady normal cry, not overanxious. It could have broken the stone walls in two.

"I'm not taking the children out here any more," its mother said to the woman beside her.

Of course, Maud thought. In all her thinking she had not realised that the waiting room would be full of women. She looked around. There were three men and dozens of women. She had not seen any of them in her march to the desk.

The woman behind the glass made phone calls. Occasionally she glanced at Maud. What would you call her, Maud wondered, this woman? A duty officer, a prison officer, a correction human, a receptionist? Maud tried to be disdainful as she picked more non-existent fluff from her jacket.

The man arrived from nowhere, startling Maud. He held out his hand.

"Miss Mannering? Michael Otto." At least that's what Maud thought he said; she wasn't going to ask him to repeat his name. "This way. It's a soupy day. Like the weather in Ireland I expect?"

The weather, the weather, the weather. Where would we be without the weather? Who needs an alphabet, language, when we've got the weather.

"No, this way. Empty the contents of your bag. I'll take that," he said, lifting Maud's camera. "Tom, put that in the office until I get her back here. Through this. No, no the sensor."

Michael Otto could get impatient. A low screech made Maud jump.

"Might be coins. Empty your pockets."

She emptied her pockets. Back again. The same screech.

"Your jewellery."

Maud took off her rings. Why were these earrings so hard

to remove? They'd never caused problems before. Maud stuffed her jewellery into her bag, handed it to an officer, stepped through the sensor, retrieved her bag. She wanted to wear her ring, but her hands were shaking too much. Tom put an invisible stamp on her hand and placed it under an ultra-violet machine.

"We'll know it's you on your way out."

Her way out? She would leave this place, could even turn back now.

"We're going to J block."

Tom straightened up, a man annoyed that a casual caller was going to see his unraked garden, his open septic tank. Tom, a comfortable homely name. You could hear a wife calling it: "Tom, your dinner's ready."

Maud followed Michael through doorways. She tried to understand the meaning of his hand signals given to men behind glass so thick it stopped all sound. More doors opened. She took short quick steps in order to keep up, a child trying to be good with the teacher on the first day at school.

"Michael, your dinner's ready."

And then they were in the main prison. They walked briskly through a mêlée of men moving about. She had not been prepared for this. The black and white street of a small town intent on its own business. Some of them looked at her, less long than they might have if Michael had not been there. An occasional one doffed his non-hat.

"To America's sweethearts, the ladies."

She had dressed right: black trousers, white shirt, ironed, grey jacket, no fluff, black walking shoes, collegiate shoulder bag. A town's main street narrowed towards the end. They took corners, she followed through a labyrinth, and now they were at an end wall.

"We're going to J Block."

"Yes, sir. Jeep's ready."

Out at the back, the jeep idled at a loading bay. The driver had one foot on the dashboard. He pulled short drags on a cigarette, snorting the smoke out through his nostrils.

"Got to give these things up."

As reliable as the weather. The jeep pulled off and began a short journey out to "there". Maud tripped out of the vehicle. She took a deep breath. She looked at Michael. After all she knew him longer than she did the driver.

"I'll call when I need you back," he dismissed the smoker. *What will you call him?* Maud squinted at the sky in memory of Oscar Wilde and his man. There are more ways than one to doff a hat.

There was another flurry of hand signs. A door silently opened. Michael and Maud stepped inside. The door closed with a tuneful click, as one might crack one's thumb and index finger to a sound of music. Maud did not jump.

"I'll take that."

Her bag was removed from her arm before she had time to hand it over.

"The whole block, we'll do the whole block."

There was much signing of books and more introductions, names that slid past Maud. She could not grasp the pleasantries.

"Right," said Michael, "this way."

Hand signals. Doors.

And then they were there. And this is how it was. Tropical heat, men in cages like battery hens. The waiting room of a human abattoir. The place of no hope between a half-life and certain death. No connection with a world that they had lost. The murdering quarter.

Someone, not Michael, said, "There will be no note taking."

Where could she have a notebook hidden?

"And there will be no speaking. No speaking at all. Got that?"

"Yes," Maud squeaked out.

"You can ask the officer questions. He may or may not answer them. You got that?"

"Yes," Maud said, her voice having gained a little pitch. All she needed was practice.

Michael and Maud began the cortège down the corridor. There were no doors, just bars on the cells. Some men had hung their towels over a few square feet of bars in an effort to grab one patch of privacy as they did their morning wash. The lights were on in most. Some were darkened, and Maud could see the shape of a man curled up at the top of a bed, facing towards the wall. One was doing press-ups. The smell of scented wash products mingled with heat as they passed one. One stared at her, giving her a new meaning to the word blank. And still they had only passed five. Maud began to register the greetings from each cell. Friendly enough to Michael.

"Howya, Jim?"

"Not bad, not bad."

"Howya, Bill?"

"Not bad, not bad."

A laugh.

"And you, sir?"

"Not bad."

"Are you back again?"

"Not yet."

There was a bend in the corridor. It was like a day girls' school cloakroom. Maud had faced the racks where the outdoor shoes were kept during the day and the indoor shoes kept overnight. But these were men that were stacked in, not shoes. Michael stopped at the bend. Maud thought it was over. It wasn't.

"We have fifty-two prisoners here in our capital case area. It is divided in three: those just in, those here longer and those whose appeals are over and dates are being set or are set. When we come to the cell with the iron sheet, he has got his date. We'll move on now."

Maud wanted to wait a moment to catch her breath. *But what does an iron sheet mean? No, he hadn't said iron sheet. Or maybe he had.* They were on the move again.

"Howya, Paul?"

"Not bad, not bad, and you, sir?"

"Not bad."

One man intently studied a large book.

"He's working on his appeal."

Michael's frantic hand signals, in reply to something Maud hadn't seen, almost caught her in the face.

"Oh, I do beg your pardon. Stand here. A prisoner is being brought to the shower. They're strip-searched before a shower. And handcuffed on the way. And strip-searched afterwards."

And so they stood outside a man's home while they waited for a handcuffed male to walk through three sets of doors. Maud turned her back on the prisoner's domestic abode, no more than twice the size of last night's queen bed. Bunk, toilet, sink, table, one shelf.

The man folded and refolded his towel and tried not to look at her. She tried not to look back. More hand signals. On the move again. More smells. More darkened cells. More towels. More greetings.

"And how are you today?"

No answer.

"Everything all right?"

No answer.

"Got everything you need?"

No answer. The prisoner moved forward an inch or two. Maud's eyes were drawn to his face, the way that this really can happen if there is a strong enough force in the face. She looked at him and held her breath at the depth of the fear that she saw there. A look can last a lifetime. There is no look when a man is dead.

"Everything all right?"

No answer.

"Got everything you need?"

"Yes," he said. "Yes." And never had such a small word had such a mountain of a lie in it.

"Good. Now, you have a good one."

Had she heard right? "Now, you have a good one."

"That's the man who has just got his date."

Maud had not seen the iron sheet or whatever, but she had had no need. The dogs of the street would know that that man's date had arrived.

We will all die, she thought, *but it will not be at an appointed day, hour, minute and by the hands of someone else.*

She had just seen the appointed hour. Let us face our eyes to the wall or to the far distance; it is better not to see close up.

"Howya, Terence?"

"Not bad, not bad."

"Now here's our medical room."

A strapping lad appeared to be joking with the doctor. His date hadn't arrived yet, obviously.

"We have good medical facilities. The prisoners can get all they need."

Indeed.

"There's our law library." There appeared to be about ten books in it. "And another library." Michael did a fast flourish of his hand but drew it back to his side again. There appeared to be five books in that one.

"And there's our barber's shop. They can have their hair cut as often as they want."

And their throats, too, if they are lucky. Maud was definitely down there now. And so the march continued. At some point another silent officer had tagged on behind Maud. Maybe it was after the shower incident, or maybe after the dead man looking, she couldn't quite remember. Michael continued to chat amicably.

"Is it hard on you?" Maud asked, suddenly. "Knowing them, and that?" Her voice was back. "When the time comes, like?"

"We're just doing our job."

That was a historical sentence.

"It is not us who do it. The court decides, the governor signs, we do as we are told."

"But does it not affect all of you, your families, the town even?"

The silent man spoke. "The officer might not want to answer that question."

But he did.

"We have counselling services. Once a month on J Block we are debriefed."

So the authorities recognise something. There is no monthly counselling for train drivers.

"And special counselling if you bring a man up. I brought the last man up."

As if he had reared him.

"The execution is not carried out here. Twenty-four hours or so before, he is brought up. I brought him up."

He said it again.

"I'm not back working yet on J block. I brought him up, rode up with him. You get time off the block after bringing a man up."

There was a musing to the last sentence, the sound of a whispered confidence shared from behind a cupped hand. Was he proud of himself that he hadn't cracked under the strain? Was he looking for sympathy? Or forgiveness? Or at least understanding?

The march ended because there is a finite length to each death row. It only takes so much space to house fifty two men, fifty one next week unless they got someone else in. Who got the man's cell, an old-timer or a newcomer? For how long did the fear hang about the bars? Could it be sprayed away with air-freshener? Near the door, Michael pointed to the solitary confinement block, where prisoners from the main prison could be housed.

"I bet that keeps them in line," Maud said, without a trace

of amusement. Or was it hiding there somewhere between the words? Michael ignored the remark. At march's end there were more hand signals and signings. There was a problem. She had put 16/4. It should have been 4/16. Watches were checked, the hour and the minute recorded.

"I'll show you the visiting area."

Someone handed her a collegiate looking shoulder bag.

"Good luck, Michael. Hurry back. When are you coming back?"

Outside, the jeep waited. The driver had one foot on the dashboard. He pulled short drags on a cigarette. It could have been the same one.

"Got to give these things up."

They drove around the block, through a desert of famished grass. One wild goose hopped around.

"She was nesting, but I think the lawn mowing has disturbed her," the driver said.

Michael showed the wired exercise cages, each big enough to hold two men.

"Never more than two. We only put compatibles in together. Some men would always have to be on their own."

They alighted from the jeep to view the visiting room. Michael opened the door into a huge barn-like interior. Built in the centre of the floor were two adjoining narrow cages, all thick glass. A fat person would have to be squeezed in. There were two people, visitors, already waiting. Both of them stared at the opening door, composing their features for a greeting.

"I'm sorry," Maud said. She waved from her waist up, truly sorry to have made their hearts jump.

"Our visitors get a few hours, once weekly. In the last

week, family or designated friends can visit daily. Some of them don't have any."

Michael closed the door and they returned to the jeep for the last lap.

They backtracked through the main prison, the town still busy with its bits and bobs, its routines.

"You never had it so good," Maud muttered.

"Still no talking."

Oh yes, no talking, no note taking. But they couldn't stop the thinking.

"As you can see, they wear different uniforms here. Two piece. A condemned man always wears a one piece jump suit."

Her hand under the ultraviolet must have shown her to be who she was. Or had been on her way in. Someone handed her a camera.

Back at the front desk, Superintendent Donald J. Calvin himself arrived to shake her hand. It was more a slide than a shake.

"You don't have the death penalty in Ireland?"

You don't have sour dough bread?

"No," Maud said. "We did once, but not any more."

"Do you think it would help?"

"Help what?"

"Of course, I can't comment myself. I do give a press statement at designated times." That would be after an execution. "You know it was off for a while when the lawyers said that it was unconstitutional. But I cannot comment overall."

"No, of course not," said Maud, mannerly to the last.

The superintendent slid hands again.

"No photographs, remember." As if she would have dared break a rule.

Michael brought her right out to the last door. There were no buttons attached to this one. He opened it wide for her, letting in a gust of real air. He shook her hand, really shook her hand.

"Goodbye," said Maud.

"Have a good one," said Michael.

CHAPTER 21

MAUD HAD DIFFICULTY getting the car started. She lit a cigarette; her hands were shaking. Perhaps she should wait until the shaking had subsided before driving off. Perhaps she would write a letter to Malachy, take the coward's way out. If she wrote a letter he could keep it, and then both he and she would remember every detail of this day. As if she could forget. She switched off the engine, deciding to finish her cigarette, took one more drag and raised her eyes to the wall. To hell with the shaking, she was getting out of here fast. All she had to do was remember to watch the side of the road. All she had to do was retrace her steps to King of Prussia, whose suburbs in fact stole up on her much sooner than she had expected.

At the car hire office they greeted her like a returned explorer. *They know*, Maud thought.

"Do you mind if I ask what you were doing at the prison?"

"How did you know?" Maud smiled, the first crease to come into her cheeks since she had kissed Gerard goodbye.

"There's nothing else there. Then I thought that no one would ask for directions there, they would ask for Collegeville. Then I thought that you weren't local so you might not know."

"I was taking photographs. I'm a photographer," Maud said.

"Interesting, interesting. That must be fun. Car all right?"

"Great."

* * *

Maud took the Greyhound bus to Philadelphia where she booked into the Holiday Express Inn, a more expensive sister of the Holiday Inn. "Nineteenth floor, no smoking, sorry, no coffee, but you can smoke on the landing of the twentieth floor." There are some death rows where smoking is not allowed. The bed had grown. Maud's throat was scraping against itself, her temperature was rising, but some of it soaked off in the large bath. It was four o'clock in the afternoon. She locked the door of the room and stayed silent for sixteen hours, idly examining the wallpaper and such.

The unknown voice was there again before waking.

"How was it?"

"If you really don't want to know, don't ask. I have seen too much to want to argue with you. I do not now have the luxury of your ignorance." That settled that. At breakfast she stole her lunch again. It wasn't really stealing.

* * *

Maud was now on the last solitary leg of her journey. The grand, tiled coolness of Philadelphia Station melted seamlessly into the shuttle to Baltimore airport. She ate her bagel and cream cheese while she waited for the delayed plane. She distracted herself by cataloguing the earringed people. "Southeast Airlines welcome aboard the passengers joining us here on this Iceland to Nashville flight. Enjoy our leather seats."

A man holding a sign with "JOURNEY" painted on it met her at the airport and brought her to accommodation for the night. She would be picked up in the morning to join the others at Knoxville. The relief of seeing a sympathetic face almost overwhelmed her. She talked too much, but he didn't seem to mind. She did it in a varied way, not monotone, and he rather liked her accent.

CHAPTER 22

BY THE TIME Maud had spent two days with the group, she thought she had the hang of it. She didn't know what to call them. The long name was ridiculous, but Journeyers might be OK. "Start shortening the journey," her father used to say when he wanted a song from the back of the car. She hung on to connections like that, trying to make sense of things, picking bits of this and that from her memory, tailends that might help, shamelessly comparing like with non-like in an effort, if not to fit perfectly, to at least sidle in, as a latecomer might in a procession or into the crowd going to Croke Park. In the morning when she woke, she tried to hold on to her own distance and thought that she would never have made a good candidate for boarding school. She found break-fast difficult, being used to the solitary act of feeding and dressing herself at the same time, in that relieved place where a person doesn't have to meet another's eyes and is apt to forget, over the Weetabix, whether the bra is on or off. She kept her shower until after breakfast, so that she could again retreat into privacy, hide under water, a fish confident of not being caught. There she scrubbed at her skin, noticing each morning that some of the jet lag was leaving her bones, that patches of the sore throat were falling away like peeled sunburn, that her temperature was settling back. Putting her clothes and face cream on in a crowded room soon became normal.

On the first day Maud had made efforts to read the lists posted each night, to see how these pieces fell together, to check names of speakers in schools, times, rotas, names to churches. To remember who had someone murdered and who was an organiser and who had a murderer for family. It was best to keep her mouth shut until she could fit stories with faces. It was not the sort of thing you asked: "Tell us, are you an organiser, or did you see your mother shot?"

She overheard the way to find out. "So what's your story? How did you become part of the journey?"

This was not often asked, because these people mostly knew each other, were annual pilgrims to the wishing well. They were tied together by a knowledge of each other normally reserved for the brightest possible intimacy. From Alaska to Florida, Kansas to New Hampshire, blood to electric chair, Nashville to Spokane, flesh to needle, Ohio to LA. They were one. Not all year. But for this particular blessed week when they didn't have to pretend.

"Who is going with Sam to Notre Dame? We have an advocate; we need somebody for literature. Put your names down on the lists. You can see who is speaking where and at what time."

The names of venues — they were called event sites — were not in Maud's normal ken. Metropolitan Interdenominational Church, Episcopalian, United Methodist, First Congregational, Friends Meeting House, Presbyterian, Unitarian, Oh! Christ Church Cathedral, Notre Dame High School, Christian Brothers. So much worshipping. Some of the names of the people were more familiar: Stephen, Bill, Sam, SueZann, Rene, George, Lois, Ken, Sally, Cathy, Celeste, Steve. Organisers: Sarah, Mariah, Tammy, Zak, Mary Ann and crossovers of all. Singers: Steve, Carol, Peewee.

"We're going to speak to the Catholic community at John XXIII. I think we should be at the mass first."

"One mass a day is enough for this Jew."

General laughter, opening a moment to allow an exchange of banter, some of which veered right to the edge.

"Right, who is driving Sam? And Maud, you will go with him. Maud is visiting us from Ireland. She was on Graterford row last week, so if anyone wants to ask her any questions, they can."

Jesus Christ. What could she say? What if it was a relative of a man there? Someone who had never seen the inside? Should she make it worse or better than it was? Maud hurried to the back of the group, hoping that no one would have seen her. Fat chance.

"So tell us, what's the weather like in Ireland now?"

"So-so."

"Don't worry. No one's going to bite you. Just go to the different speakers and hear their stories. You'll get into the swing of it. It's good for the speakers to have someone with them in case things get rough. You'll come in useful."

So Maud signed up and trouped to schools, churches, lecture theatres, parks, concerts, demonstrations. She got in and out of cars and vans, had tea with priests and pastors, listened with both ears open when required, closed one or half closed both when the exhaustion of constant moving and listening and thinking made people's conversation hollow and tired.

* * *

Her name was SueZann.

"I was in the living room with my father the night that a crazed madman broke into our house and stabbed him twenty-four times. I was stabbed four times. I have a plate here."

She touched the soft spot to the right of her eye. Hers was metal hard. Her eyes were soft. She cut hair for a living and ran her fingers through the heads of her customers, attracting oils they didn't know that they had to the surface of their scalps. She daydreamed while doing this. She could still wink, but forgot details of things at times. Forgiveness was the best tonic anyone had ever given her. It was a mysterious gift that had allowed her to laugh again. She had fought for ten years to get the killer off death row. She did not want his blood on her hands. He could stay in prison for ever for all she cared, but she did not want to be party to his murder. And she did forgive him. Who was Maud to argue? SueZann carried a bible with her and got people to sign it. It was to be a present for him. Someday he would let her visit him. Of this she was sure. She saw his name everywhere, not all the time, she said, but during this week a lot: Reid Street, Christopher Park, that sort of thing. She had seen the knife the last time, he had lifted it; she had heard her father, had seen him try to drag himself across the floor. She had lived. She owed her father. For him she would forgive, that was what he had taught.

"Would you like your hair cut, Maud? I'll do it after the last school."

She was a slight woman. She had to wear tight jeans with the shirt tucked inside, because it would have been a terrible waste not to show off such a perfect shape. She laughed a lot, now that she had remembered how. It could be picked out from among others, a wide sound, the dust of cigarettes in it. If people were busy talking at one end of the room and heard that laugh, they wished they were near it. Sunday every day of the week. When she did Maud's hair, she pushed her neck forward, and bones went off like crackers down to Maud's spine. She let two tears fall on to her lap, then straightened herself up. She went to hear more.

* * *

It was hard to concentrate on the country outside. Maud couldn't decide if this was because all strangeness merges into one big unfamiliarity or because the hearing of the stories shut out the sense of sight. The rolling hills were there, lapping up one to one, travelling out to the far distance, millions of trees waving into each other, blues competing in a bouquet of brightness. On rounding some bends, a playroom of hoarding signs engulfed the vista.

* * *

His name was Sam.

"My mother was murdered by an intruder when I was seven. She put me to bed, but someone else picked me up out of my sleep while it was still dark and rushed me past the living room door which was covered with a sheet. There were a lot of strange men in our living room. At the door the first camera flashes of my life blinded me. I couldn't get the sleep from my eyes. My father was accused."

He would have been like Harry, waiting for them to see the wrongness of that action — just a mistake, a dreadful mistake, but it would be all right — confident in his innocence. Sam's father would have been appalled by this mistake but more taken up with grief for his dead wife. Harry would not have had too much of that. Neighbours only live near by, not in your heart. They took Sam, the child, to an uncle's house. He could not go to his mother's funeral because of the cameras. He feared cameras. The departments mucked each other up, and with each day's headlines, the intruder got further away, the truth was run over, and his father went to jail. In the negotiated mire of hatred, his father was too good looking, too white. He wasn't hateable enough to send him to the execution chamber.

The child was an expert on the manual jump search that preceded electronic bleeps. Down a corridor, two large men jumped out of the dark and frisked him, under the arms, in the crevices of the body that belong to the person alone, the unreachable places where a tick might hide. To this day he carries that expertise with him; it singles him out, makes security men always want to search him, the smell of it is a challenge to them. The cameras stayed, the film crews came, his home address belongs to the world, not him. He has not been back to his home. The pictures of his dead mother are a product and belong to you and me more than to him. He is afraid of cameras. A child's lifetime later his father was freed, innocent still, at last, always. But it wasn't his father; it was not the man that could have been. He died four years later, not yet having reached comfortable middle age, a man pursued by greasy newsmen and cameras.

The child retreated and remained a recluse until flames, smoke and sparks shot six inches out of the head of Jessie Tafero, as three 2000-volt shocks of incorrect amperage were administered, bungled so the flesh cooked on his bones before he died. The man was innocent as convicted, as it so happens. The child man came out of the woods and speaks now in a soft, loud voice so that people are moved. He was asked to appear on a television show to discuss The Case. He refused. It had the word "Entertainment" in its title. Always The Case. Never the false imprisonment of his father. There is no legal word for a farce. Carnival, circus has been used. It is not good enough. This man wants a lexicographer. The Case is taught in media classes. It gave an ailing paper one hundred days of saleable headlines and saved it from bankruptcy. It made millionaires of film producers.

* * *

The pastors made a circle, they closed their eyes, held hands and prayed to God. This clasping lasted many minutes. Occasionally a short prayer would burst forth like the spark from a burning cinder. Maud's embarrassment knew no bounds. The two clergymen on either side of her retrieved their wet hands when the time was up. Maud hadn't heard who called it if it was called at all. Maybe God, but she couldn't hear him; he had never been on the same frequency as her. She frequently didn't hear the calling of times in pubs either.

* * *

Her name was Lois Robinson.

"We are an average family except that our son is on death row in Texas. Here is his picture. He was a son that anyone would have been proud of. Larry was diagnosed as a paranoid schizophrenic at the age of twenty-one. We tried in vain to get him proper treatment. We were told that he would get worse without it. He was routinely discharged after thirty day stints because they needed the bed. And he had not been violent. Not yet. We were told that if he became violent he could get the long-term treatment that everyone agreed he needed."

Lois and Ken, his mother and father, pleaded to have him left in hospital.

When asked if he had been violent, they always said that, no, he had not.

"If only we had lied," they whispered together.

He finally exploded and killed five people. He was found to be sane and sentenced to death. Hospital records were passed over as if they were nearby mirages. Lois had transparent skin. She and Ken were only thirty-six years married and couldn't keep their arms from around one another. She taught school, he teaches Spanish at college, gets lost in dreams of other places. He wanted a photograph of Maud. Lois couldn't find a post-box to post a letter to her son. Someone would go look. They did that kind of thing.

* * *

That evening a tree was to be planted at a church. The congregation met them at the door, solid men and women singing songs for talk. The food was made, lots of it, but later. A pastel-skinned female, dressed in a purple jumper, black hanging swishing skirt and a flowered hat came to the front. *Holy cow*, thought Maud. *Miss Southern Belle*. The belle was the minister. *Holy Jesus*. The minister raised a voice to God for help. "Amen," said Maud. The minister looked as if she had come from an age less rude than this one. A pear tree was produced, the hole was dug, and a circle was made. Then that thing again, the holding of hands. Maud couldn't get used to it. Worse still, she could now feel the electrical current running from one to the other. She lowered her eyes. But either she was getting used to it, despite herself, or this one was over before she noticed, three steps of a dance slipped in while making hay. Each person left their spot and dropped clay on the tree, touching it as they passed, saying the name of a loved one out loud. Maud watched. That should be easy enough. A woman stooped with a child in her arms. She closed her eyes to think her thought, and the child picked up a handful of dirt and ate it. Everyone laughed. The singers sang, a mother and a son first. And then Steve, the one with the edges. A voice soaked, with a shadow in it. Now they cried, and everyone would know why. They dusted their hands, hugged tight, even Maud, and went to eat.

Next day the woman came. Maud had heard her name: "Is Sunny coming? When Sunny comes . . . You'll meet Sunny." Sonia for real, Sunny for truth. Her back was so straight it was crooked in the opposite direction. Her laugh was as dirty as they come. When she was young, she behaved like she was young. She fell in love with a man with a past. He fell in love with her. Maud wondered what she would have been like then. His choice of friends was not the best. Outside a car in which they had slept, waiting for morning to come so that they could collect money that was owed, start a new life, a fight broke out between the suddenly arrived cops and the friend of Sunny's husband. Sunny threw herself on top of her children, one seven years old and one ten months old. Her husband lay face down on the bonnet of the car, hands behind his head, legs apart. She heard the shots. The shooter worked out a plea, two for one. She, too, did not believe that this could happen.

For five years she stayed alone on death row, no other woman even to shout at. Now there are more, not then. Five years in a single cage. She meditated and yogaed her way to sanity. Her body was the tool to keep her mind alive. She learned yoga from television. There was her and the box, breathing, stretching, emptying, and meals shoved through a hole without a word. She was then given life without parole. The judge had known that this should have been the case in the first instance, but what the heck, he would cool her heels for a while, teach her not to have a husband with dodgy friends. She forgives the judge, because she doesn't want to waste the time hating him. And ten more years in ordinary jail, a letter a day between husband and wife, how to make love without touching.

Then the execution of Jessie Tafero, her husband, the man with his face down on the bonnet, his hands behind his head. The man whose death took Sam from the hills. Two more years. It is found that neither she nor the dead he could have fired the shots. She comes out to a place outside. She knows her husband, the letter writer, should be by her side. She wishes he was here. She has not gone to his grave, doesn't want to think of him like that. She doesn't think that she will ever go. She lives with the grown daughter who was once ten months old. Her son has a son. Her parents are dead. She went to prison a child, a wife, a mother. She came out an orphan, a widow, a grandmother. She empties out her breath, lifts up her face and rolls into that laugh. There are now two laughs not easily forgotten.

* * *

Maud detached herself from the emotion. She went to her bed in the corner to study statistics. This would be Malachy's way. At school he had longed for the passover to algebra after Keats. Keats was OK for girls, and some boys, of course. He didn't mean it. Could she not take a joke?

"Maud, what are you thinking about?"

"Keats and his Odes."

> *Fade far away, dissolve, and quite forget*
> *What thou among the leaves hast never known,*
> *The weariness, the fever and the fret*
> *Here, where men sit and hear each other groan . . .*

In the corner, two of the organisers painted slogans for the demonstration. Blue and red on white. They used statistics and one-liners. She would join this painting. It was lucky that she had been to a demonstration once before.

One innocent person discovered and released for every six executions done.

Half death row population comes from 18 per cent of the population's colour.

One third of death row population is mentally ill or deformed.

They closed the hospitals, made jails. The patients are back.

Why do we kill people who kill people to show that killing people is wrong?

Execution is not the solution.

Don't kill for me.

It's still murder.

Thou shalt not kill.

Not in my name.

Not in my state.

An eye for an eye leaves the whole world blind.

She presumed that Malachy would have liked the slogans. How could she think that? He had never given the subject any consideration whatsoever, had never been introduced to it, was blissfully ignorant still. They propped the placards in a corner and got ready for an evening at the university. Tonight was party night, they chanted. Maud had her doubts. She would have to drink slowly.

* * *

They lined up beer and, thankfully, some wine. The speedily produced well-being of drink sent them into fast talking. There was no death here. Drops of stories were flittered out as a good card dealer might idly throw the pack around. They broke into groups of two, three, four. They talked of their lives at home. They could have been a crowd of conference goers, were in a way. But the people within earshot of their dropped familiarities would not have wanted to join them.

"Maud, do your parents live in Dublin?"

"No, they're dead." Dead was daily currency here.

"How?"

"Just an ordinary death. A car crash."

She refrained from telling them about Harry. She was afraid that it might seem like an irrelevant history, too long ago; afraid that they might feel that she was trying to tie herself to their recent grief. There was a question as to what she was doing here. It had no answer yet. She was glad that the speakers needed a listener guaranteed to be on their side, glad there were placards to be made.

A man may have made an attempt to seduce Maud, he would have been entitled, but Maud was terrified. What if it wasn't a pass? What if the signal was a key down from that? If she got it wrong, if her response tipped into the wrong place, she would never forgive herself, should never forgive herself. And if he was trying to seduce her? How could she sleep with a man whose life was piled so high with loss? Maybe he was just loafing about with her in this stolen hour. Maybe he just liked her accent. She was on the verge of inventing a husband-to-be, which could technically be a truth, when the call went out that the vans were leaving. He made certain of being in the same one as her; she made certain of not sitting beside him. She could hear her voice in her ears. She hoped it hadn't become too young, too carnival-time.

Practising barber shop singers back at their church hall translated the language of love into high notes and deflated them out into the air where they became undangerous. They sang like choir boys, out of sync with their years, amused at the perfection of their pitches. Then they excused themselves.

They needed privacy for proper practice; a public should not hear discordant notes. The Journeyers drifted to the various corners where their beds lay. There was packing to be done for the early start. What would the next accommodation be like? This was a big question. They opened the doors of new places like students opened exam papers.

Within hours of leaving, the places they stayed became objects of reminiscence, as if they had been lovers of a long duration. The bad bits were left out. Too dark and dismal, a little scary, but the showers were good. Co-ed toilet, all those stairs, but the morning sun streamed into the basketball room that was their shared bedroom. Maud dried her clothes on the hot spots on the floor. Mattresses too lumpy, a noise like a nearby fart going off half hourly, but there was a clothes line and a public phone. Last place too crowded, only two feet between beds, but everything else was perfect.

Maud learned to undress without being seen. And to sleep to the varied pitches of snoring, usually contemptible in her opinion. But they came from the mouths of these people. They had to be excused. These were the mouths that repeated those stories, tore those memories from their guts and laid them out on slabs for the ignorant to pick at. In the name of education. They were entitled to snore the snores of the innocent.

CHAPTER 23

IT WAS A Thursday morning after a late breakfast. Maud
thought that she was lonely, but it could have been over-
load. There was still a lot of hugging. Some people closed
tight, briefly, only when they needed it, but one or two
prowled around looking to see if there was a spare one going
and if they could insinuate themselves into it. Yet despite the
abundance of wraparound handshakes, she felt untouched.
She was used to this, kept telling herself that she was well used
to this, but still she felt deprived. It was language really. The
speed that one is allowed. And the words that one can use
without explanation. And the pitch. It was the taste of crackers. And the sight of lizards. And the fact that no one here
cared what the girls in the office were doing, had no interest
in their names or when she went on her last date. She hadn't

realised that Majorie and Caitríona had crept so closely up into her life. Accident of circumstance, work. The perfect place to divulge just so much and no more. There was a great freedom in the no more place, and yet a strong loyalty in the so much. Maud bought an international dialing card and made her way to a public phone. She couldn't telephone her work, that would have been a break of etiquette too far. But she could ring Malachy.

"Hello," he said, his voice sounding as if it was half of hers. "Well, how's Tennessee?"

"Beautiful really. Bright at the moment, but quite chilly. The bars in Nashville were full of music, as you'd expect. Strange town, old old taxies, where you can still smoke. Imagine."

"Indeed. Well, nothing's changed here. Valerie is going to take up a picture framing class. She says that she knows enough not to be a weekend painter, but framing would be all right. Have you seen anything interesting?"

"Well, I went on this tour from Chattanooga. The guide knew the ins and outs of every battle. You know the Confederates and all that. She had a very serious philosophy of forgiveness, what it does to a person. They have got the first National Military park. She thought that when her mother's murderer got the death penalty that she would feel perfect, that the closure thing would happen to her, but instead she felt worse and realised that execution only prolonged the agony."

"I think, Maud, if you don't mind my saying so, you're supposed to be on your holidays. You should leave the Department of Justice to run itself."

"Oh yeah, you're right. Miniature golf was invented here on Lookout Mountain in 1928. The Tom Thumb course was the first in the world. We went to hear a speaker. You could roll around in the pronunciation of his Rs. New Hampshire, I think. You know the way they speak."

"What were you doing going to hear a speaker? What kind of speaker?"

"History, a history of the place. There are more than three hundred kinds of trees and nine hundred varieties of wild flowers in the Chattanooga area, more than anywhere else on the earth except central China."

"Ah yes. Good. Was it interesting?"

"Did I not say? Yeah, yeah, really interesting. His father was. . . sorry, bad line there. Yes, there are lectures any evening you want."

"Gosh, I would never have thought of Tennessee as that sort of place."

"The New Hampshire fellow was really into the hugs. I wouldn't have minded one myself."

"Maud, are you all right? Maud, are you sure you're OK?"

"Yeah, yeah."

"Well, you don't sound that great. Is the holiday relaxing you?"

"Oh yeah, yeah." She seemed to be made up of yeahs. "Listen, Malachy, I've got to go. This card is running out."

"We'll pick you up at the airport."

"No, no, please don't. I'll make my own way."

She hated the way they bundled in on top of her just when she wanted some privacy. Just a few hours to look at Dublin, to check her journey home, to see how low the skyline went. Just to be able to walk into her own flat alone, to reacquaint herself with the dribble of water that passed for a shower, to realise that it was adequate. And then when she needed them, or rather Malachy, they would be totally unavailable.

"No, no. Of course, we'll pick you up. Valerie said to say so, if you rang."

"OK, OK."

And it would be good to see them. To leave all this behind, hide more secrets. When she saw Malachy, she would know what to say.

"So. Cheerio. See you then."

"Thanks for ringing."

Malachy put down the phone. He sat on the couch and wondered. Had he talked enough to Maud since their parents died? Is it possible for someone to become unhinged gradually before your very eyes? Could a person be too busy with telling old stories to a new love, with putting forward plans one on top of the other? If he and Valerie got married, would he then have more time to spend with Maud? Or would the time be different? And if so, would that be a good or a bad thing?

Maud walked back up the Chattanooga sidewalk, back to the church hall. On the steps, the non-smokers sat with the smokers, sniffing vicarious pleasure and wearing self-right-eousness. They were getting tired. Manners could snap here, as people longed to be home, longed not to have to trot out their own stories.

"I wonder could the people leaving early in the morning not flush the toilet. Some of the people still in bed are the ones who have spoken latest last night. They need to sleep late."

No problem, everyone agreed. Then someone had to get all excited about a new rule. "And do you know what else we could do. . ."

Jump in a lake, Maud thought. Maud would not have been able to explain her exasperation. She could think swear words into her mouth — shove it, fuck it, things she didn't usually think — but she couldn't let them out. She should have told Malachy.

"I have a reaction to the smell of your aftershave. Do you think you could not use it, or at least not use so much of it?"

"Tell you what, I'll use what I damn well like, but I'll stay away from you until it's worn off. The others can smell me to see how close I should get to you."

"They'll be able to do that in one of those embraces," Maud said, letting the thing slip out, the way a secret could. This could have caused extreme silence. Instead everyone laughed. It must have been her accent. They regrouped to continue teaching. One of the organisers was getting into a harridan mode. She wore a face like thunder. *Yet thunder never did me that much harm*, Maud thought. At work or in her own city, she would have had choices. Avoid, confront, wheedle. But she was not in her own city. And would not be for another four days. She got up from the steps, even though she wanted another cigarette, and walked to where her bed was. Her back was still straight, but a weight was dragging her shoulders down, and her eyes were getting dull.

She seemed to be lucky, usually getting the corner of the room. She hid down in her sleeping bag and took out the airport thriller. It was not the sort of book one could read full-frontal here. Under the covers she ticked off personality types and wondered how many types there were in the world. She drifted into sleep and dreamt that she was burying her father. Not her mother. When the priest was finished, she asked if he would then perform the wedding of herself and her boyfriend.

"*What?? Now!!*" The boyfriend screamed.

"Stop moaning," Maud said. "We'll get both over and done with in one go."

She sat bolt upright in the strange bed. Was it possible that she could be that cruel? Who was the boyfriend? There was no face left. Pity. She wondered if she knew him.

She got out of bed quickly. "I'm making for the kitchen," she said to Carol, "to get something sweet quickly. Sugar or suicide."

That was the terrible thing about crowds, you always had to explain yourself. A woman in the kitchen was persuading people to eat more. Maud's mother had been like that, would never let people out of the house without eating. *Do you remember, Malachy?* She had begun to converse regularly with Malachy. It was an old habit. She slipped into it like a gambler would slide into a bookies. The mood in the kitchen was bright. Sometimes it was like that, a sudden beam coming from somebody, caused by heaven knows what, lighting up those around them, lifting the voices a semi-tone. And then they could hear the laughs from the other end of the room.

Tomorrow would be Maud's last day. She must not start counting the hours. She could let her mind wander again, that would help. She did this at work sometimes, but not often, being mostly satisfied with her job. She was satisfied with it now. The Department of Justice, despite the quibbling done at tea break, did at least pass a glancing tribute to the word. Somewhere the ethos did embrace justice, justice did include second chances, people were not glad that the prisons were filling up.

The clashes of venom were not as sharpened as they were here. All of which was an odd thing for Maud to think, considering her recently discovered history. But that was then.

"A penny for them?"

"I just think that in other places people believe that the loss of freedom is the punishment. But here that's only the start. We also believe in parole. Not a cat playing with a mouse. We actually believe in the dictionary definition. In order to do that, you have to accept that a prisoner can promise, and can aspire to good behaviour. In order to believe that, you must think that a prisoner is human. Here people don't believe that. To err is to be not human. This is a hard place, no concessions are given. For all the wealth there is little leeway."

"Surely you never thought that wealth gave leeway."

"I didn't know. Honestly, I didn't know."

Maud felt immensely sad, because somehow she had believed that wealth did give leeway. If a person has so much, why do they not want to give a little? In truth, Maud had not met enough wealthy people to understand that having was keeping, and keeping was keeping out. She did that thing again, that thing she did when everything got too much. Lists. The insults to shout from a hilltop to a boyfriend if you had a boyfriend. You make way too much noise eating. You drop your clothes everywhere. I hate the way you lower your voice when you drink, then I can't hear you. But she only got to three. And realised that there was always the radio to cover the noise, and she didn't mind tidying at all. And if she couldn't hear him, then she would have to get closer. She was truly making an effort to divert herself. *Malachy, I am trying, I am trying.* One more day to go.

In the morning they straggled outside to a bright light to wait for transport. They grouped like people waiting for a sports outing to begin. Maud was particularly magnanimous, in the way that departure makes a person be. She helped with everything: placards, water bottles, leaflets, the old women and men. The bus arrived to take them to her last march. Maud walked away to take a photograph. They, the Journeyers, were lined up outside as if they were at school, trauma school, how it's not supposed to have turned out school. Yet they looked like survivors. They understood the non-uniformity of their laughs, and their clothes were individual; they had been acquired by themselves to fit.

They moved on to the bus, taking their own time to get their feet up, breathing in and out with the effort of what this march might throw up. A victims' group was rumoured to be on its way. Its members sometimes accused this group of not caring for their murdered kin because they did not believe in execution. The bus driver weaved his way quietly through the streets. The light shone as it always did. This would be a day for holidays in another place. A sign on the motorway asked, DOES THE ROAD YOU ARE ON LEAD YOU TO MY PLACE? SIGNED GOD. A week ago she would have laughed. But now one thing made as much sense as another. She picked out other signs, searching for places to put her mind, as if it was a spreadable sheet to be laid out flat on the grass when there was no more room on the clothes line — that's what her mother had done. And hid her uncle, which was why Maud was now on this bus.

They disembarked, released and tense. They took more photographs. Hers would be hard to explain if she ever let them spill out accidentally in the office. Stewards lined them in threes, put the slowest walkers to the top and urged them to limber up their voices. Lunch hour was explained.

"We need to get the message across to the office workers. Shout from the diaphragm if your throat is getting hoarse. Shout loud."

Under her breath, Maud practised what a shout like that might be like if it was let out. They moved off and picked up a rhythm, both in their feet and their mouths. No one heckled, being forced to silence by the moral authority of the marchers. Some bystanders did snort. A few turned their backs. Keep moving; this is a demonstration, not an argument. One tin can was thrown. The marchers skipped over it. The chant took away the bounce of its sound.

Underneath the town hall the speakers took their two minutes each and did with them what they could. The sun got hot. The churches came on. A bishop said that the churches and the therapeutic community had dropped the ball. His voice boomed higher than a helicopter sound.

"Execution is not a punishment," he said; "it is a crime."

One by one they placed themselves before the microphone and put their money where their mouths were.

"Remember that one in six we execute is probably innocent. We are not winning. This is not a popular campaign. We merely hold the line until the children can take over."

Maud moved beneath a tree. Her head was hot. A large black Protestant bishop with a historical booming voice full of warmth and warning called for a round of applause for the pope, the man who had welcomed a thousand of these marchers into St Peter's Square, the churchman who had spoken, whose lead must be followed. The clap grew louder and louder, three cheers for the pope. Could she do it? If she rubbed her palms together quickly, would that count? She had to light a cigarette.

When they were young, Maud had argued against confession, but Malachy had said that it was a fine idea. He said that a person had a right to be forgiven. "It makes people lazy about being good," Maud had said. "Balderdash," Malachy replied. He might have clapped if he had been here today. The singer with the shadows sang his song, written for a man who had asked him to attend his death. The singer described the death. Maud put her fingers in her ears. The man had wanted one person who didn't hate him to be in the room. The death rattle was loud. The singer described the death certificate. Homicide, it said. The singer sang the short song. A single bird answered him; the helicopter moved off. The singer moved forward on his toes and smiled. The crowd clapped.

News came through about Delaware. They had just done their first in thirty-five years. The man had murdered his wife and child. The remaining child had pleaded with the governor for his father's life. But the governor knew better. The man had somehow got a knife and tried to fight the warders who were bringing him up. It was not just how he'd got the knife that shocked people, it was the fact that he fought. No one expected it, wishing to believe that the men and women walking to their deaths acquiesce in the march and do not want to fight for their lives. Perhaps they knew that this could not be true, but they wished. And wished that the news from Delaware could be sent back.

The marchers got back on their bus and returned to the church basement. The cook had a meal ready. She had once been in Ireland, "of all places", she said, so in honour of Maud she had boiled the water to boiling point and had a teapot. After the last meal Maud packed her belongings, folding her clothes neatly, although she didn't need to do so. The next time she would see them would be at the door of her own washing machine. There was the same space in her suitcase as when she had arrived. She had bought no presents. She hoped that there was a decent shop at the airport. She closed her bag.

They came out to see her off. The names came to her, one by one, as she hugged some and kissed some, most on the cheek, two near the mouth. Everyone hates goodbyes. But these people in particular. She could feel the scar tissue on their cheeks. The driver brought her to the airport, her mind already on the next school.

Maud felt a thousand thoughts. Mostly that heretofore she would never be the same, that she might never plop into sleep again, that the news could not be sent back. First Philadelphia, King of Prussia, Norristown, Pottstown, Collegeville, Bethlehem, Graterford. Then Nashville, Monteray, Oakridge, Chattanooga, Chickamauga. All across Tennessee she had done her best not to fall apart. It was time to go. Home.

Maud walked away from the bus. There was no one running behind her, trying to catch up.

CHAPTER 24

BACK AT HOME, Maud had slipped perfectly into her routine within three weeks. Every morning she woke, thrilled to be in her own bed. The list of changes that she had made, to pass time on the flight home, was already in the bin. Major things needed to be done — furniture shifting, out of season spring cleaning, conversation with Malachy — but Maud was gratifyingly empty of purpose. She began walking to work in the mornings, dawdling over her desk, buying trashy magazines, lengthening her tea breaks and devising a social calendar. If she had paid more attention to that and less to the paper round of her desk life, she might be in the suburbs by now.

She pictured herself there. The solidity and grandeur of it was overwhelming. She rattled around in wealthy smugness,

unscathed by even a hint of compassion. Her and her mythi-
cal husband's success galvanised them against the world. Her
husband, she could never quite get the physical proportions
clear, but she could smell his presence, was a quiet man, which
was just as well. He had nothing much to say about anything.
He was wealthy and faintly surprised that, while sitting on the
couch, he was making money. As his wife built up the faults
of all and sundry, he was aware that this made them better
than others. Presumably that was the point of the exercise. She
also organised the spending of his money well; he expected
that from her. But Maud got bored surprisingly fast. She lolled
about in the picture for a week or so, the length of a decent
holiday, and then erased it. Perhaps she would use bits of it
later? Who knew, but for the moment it just wasn't interesting.
Perhaps there was something wrong with her? Perhaps her
ambitions for domesticity had not grown up? And yet she did
long for something more than the passing satisfaction of office
acquaintanceship, the overpoliteness borne of necessity.

Maud ate a lot, scrambled eggs with ham and cheese on
toast in the morning, an extra sandwich at lunchtime, her
mother's stacked-up dinners in the evening. She grew a comforting stomach; it peeped out over the top of her pants. A
layer of protection appeared below the contours of her bra.
It would all have to be got off soon, but not yet. She went
drinking with Majorie and Caitríona and lied trippingly
about her time in America. She was in need of something,
should have been looking for it, but preferred to sleep late at
the weekends and potter around in loose fitting clothes that
had body parts worn into them and did nothing to make her
want to go outside.

On the fifth Saturday she lay in bed, idly feeling her rib cage and thinking of other things. She found an extra bone, or if it wasn't, then her ribs were joined off to the side of her chest plate and didn't meet directly in the middle. Imagine if that hadn't been found out until she was dead.

In all honesty, she had to admit, she needed a boyfriend or a lover or whatever a woman of her age should call him. There was a man at work, Frank. He looked at her sometimes. In the lunch queue he had once stood one eighth of an inch nearer her than was necessary. But then the next time he had kept his distance. And she had caught him looking at someone else the same way. It meant nothing. Maybe he used total eye contact with all and sundry as armour. People would have him down as a flirt, so no one would bother. That look was all very well, but imagine if you wanted him for yourself. Imagine if you had grown used to each other and he was still looking like that at everyone else. She was not ready for the exposure that love would bring. Imagine waiting for phone calls. And losing privacy with the passing hours. Ringing other people because the waiting would get her nerves on edge. Then realising that the phone had been engaged all evening. Convincing herself that that was what had happened. Planning the weekend, when now was what was wanted. Afraid to go out, afraid to stay in.

But she was ready for something. Hadn't she shared a taxi with that Frank fellow from work last Christmas? Gosh, she had forgotten.

CHAPTER 25

WHEN FRANK SHREENAN asked the young instructor on the telephone how he might go about learning to deep water dive, he was cheerily told, "Well, first we'll have to see if your body would be able for it."

"OK," he said quickly, "I'll get back to you soon."

The thought that his body might be incapable of doing something that he had just decided to do came as a big shock. He was over forty, a thing that had happened without him really noticing. He remembered being eighteen, twenty, twenty-nine and thirty-two, but the last number of years seemed to have crept up and over him. He had been waiting for something to happen, and nothing much had. Of course, he had been in love a few times, but nothing had really worked out. Either he was too pushy or not interested enough, in which

case he thought that the woman was too pushy. It was all to
do with mood, he reckoned, and it was well nigh impossible
to get two people in comparable moods for the requisite beginning. Compatibility, or equal enthusiasm, was essential at the
start, presumably for three or four months, maybe longer. He
didn't know, three or four months being the longest that he
had ever lasted. After that length of time, he was more or less
sustained enough to leave the whole process alone for half a
year or so. Except, of course, the twice that he had been badly
unsettled. After both those occasions he had stayed away from
liaisons for over a year. He often thought that maybe all that
was needed was distance and a store of good lines. His lines
appeared to become clichés before the air had dried on them.

Then Maud happened, if that's what you could call it.
Frank saw her in the canteen. He sometimes idly tried to think
about how he would describe her if he had to do so. He
couldn't really, because it wasn't the look of her that halted
him, it was more the vibrancy, the wide aliveness of her, which
came from the sum of her features. They met properly at the
Christmas party, but she wasn't the type for casual kissing, or
else she wasn't interested in him, he thought ruefully, because
that night he was really, really in the mood. And yet, later in
the nightclub, when he had a few chances with other women,
the way that no strings things are allowed to happen then, he
chose to remain untied, and instead he chastely shared a taxi
home with Maud. She took him in for coffee, and it was definitely coffee. After fifteen minutes, she said quickly, "Good
God, it's not that time. I'm away to bed. I'll see you tomorrow,
if you make it. Will I ring for a taxi or will you walk?"

And now here they were, sitting opposite each other in a

talking pub. She was drinking glasses of Guinness, he pints. She was wearing a long dress with a jumper over it; when she stood up you could see the contours of her legs through the material. Maud was totally unaware of this. Frank thought about it, and hoped that she would go the toilet soon, so that he could watch her. She did.

She looked at her face in the mirror, not really seeing herself, idly running her hand through her hair, trying to create an uncombed look. She wanted his company, that was it. She wanted him to give her some time, she even wanted a guarantee of that time, but she didn't want to go to bed with him. She could have, but she didn't. Because if she did the whole thing might be ruined. *Well, we'll see*, she thought to herself below her breath.

Back in the bar, conversation was getting louder and faster. People bumped into each other on the way to and from the counter. The weekend was beginning to build its own rhythm and smell. Tongues were loosening, confidences were wisely, and unwisely, being shared. In one corner, conversation was no longer two way; one monologist had won, eyes were glazing over, feet were shifting. Perhaps some of them would go soon and there would be a few spare stools, because it was they who would have to go. The soloist had now galloped away on the sense of his own importance. There would be no pulling him back. In another corner, a hearty storyteller had her audience eating out of her hand, except for one man who moved impatiently from foot to foot. He hated these generalisations of women. Half the time you wouldn't know what they were thinking. Well, if it was this, he didn't want to know. He tried to think of a suitable retort, a quick one-liner that would be a put down but would also be funny. And where would he slip it in? But she was too fast for him. As soon as he'd got one, she was away off on another tangent, widely unconnected with the main part of the story. This was bad for his blood pressure. He should go on home now to his wife; he would do that. As he moved away, Maud got a good view of the woman. She was green eyed and red-headed. She was amazed to find herself the centre of such rapt attention and would need to watch that she didn't overdo it.

Another customer shifted places. Maud couldn't see the woman now, but she could hear spurts of laughter coming from the spot. People stopped each other going to and from the toilets, exchanged short sentences, checking-in phrases. The more popular tried to pull away from those who would steal some of their time if they could. Some of their souls, to be exact. They did a quick eyeshift, often a perfunctory nod, but tried to smile enough so that they wouldn't be totally envied. Envied could easily become despised. They behaved as if they would be standing for elections someday. Some people bent their heads and let things be said into their ears.

Frank, too, looked at people now. The growing busyness of the pub allowed them to draw back the focus from each other. It had been a near thing — one Maud was glad she had avoided. There was a familiarity about Frank. He made her feel liked. She knew now for certain that they could have fallen over each other, but that it was a better thing not to do so. She was glad. Frank felt the barrier being erected and decided to settle for less. He was surprised that this did not annoy him and gratified to feel that something else was being born here this evening. Ten years ago, when the showing-off was at its height and people kissing on the street slapped him with envy, he would not have been content with as little as this. He didn't notice people kissing on the street so often now.

They could overhear comfortably the three women at the next table. They were trying to build to twenty the ways a person could tell her mother that she was pregnant.

"My cousins were wild. Their mother was giving the younger one a hard time about keeping late nights, the smell of drink and cigarettes, the easy downfall, the way a name could stick to a girl, the way fair-weather friends were not the best. The other one was glad that no attention was falling on her. The younger one squirmed for as long as she could take it, then reached for a cruel defence: 'Well, at least I'm not pregnant like her.'"

There was a roar of laughter and an "Oh, shit."

Someone else's friend had rung from the airport. She was going away for a mere three days, but the act of it had given her courage.

"I'm pregnant."

"God knows, Patricia, you were always very easy led. Who told you that nonsense?"

She was four months gone.

More laughter. By the time they had told these two stories, the steam had run out of the game. They would never get to twenty. Maud and Frank became diverted, but returned to pick up slices of further chat. The women were on to dreams. What could they possibly mean? If any of them needed to go to the toilet, they would wait, reluctant to miss out on this examination that might or might not make some extra sense of themselves or add an exotic reason for why they behaved the way they did.

Maud liked the fact that Frank eavesdropped on the dreams conversation. She was now absolutely sure that she could have enjoyed being locked in with him, their hearts spinning together, but equally sure that less would do, and that she would have it. Which could have been an overconfident thing to think. But Maud had second sight about that kind of thing because she had not been born alone, and this had stood to her all her life, marked her out in good and bad ways. She had someone else to remember for her. Scraps and fragments could always be checked. She could survive the entry of other people on to her horizons. Valerie was causing only manageable problems. It was all the more striking then that she still postponed her conversation with Malachy. Was she afraid to find out that perhaps they truly could view a major thing from opposite sides? And was she afraid that he would put the American examination down to sheer madness? Soon. Soon. Here in this pub she felt worn down by the secret. She thought briefly about the last year. A flash of it almost made her weak. It planked her down heavily with facts.

Frank wondered what was going on. Maud came and went. First that diving instructor git had questioned his bodily capacities, and now he definitely was not going to get off with Maud. Not only was he not going to get off with her, she faded in and out on him. But when she was in, it was worth it. It was as if she sailed away from the important parts, the rumours of communication, but became fully committed when something signalled to her attention that this might lead somewhere. But where did she want to go? She wouldn't look at him. Her eyes caught his in a speedy ball game sort of way, but rested only on his cheekbone. He knew if he could get her to look at him for a few seconds longer things might change. He also knew that he wasn't going to succeed. But in some way he was glad, because he wasn't sure if he had the spare energy to go clipping after her.

A brief exchange wafted over to them. It hit them as if it had come round the bend in a hurry.

"How's your daughter? God, she's all grown up now, I bet."

"She passed away, I'm afraid."

"Oh, my God, that's terrible. I'm terribly sorry, I'm awfully sorry."

"It's OK, it's OK. It does come as a shock to people, and I don't like being the one who has to say it all the time, but I cannot pretend that it hasn't happened."

"What happened?"

"Pregnancy complications."

"Oh, I didn't know that she was married."

"I didn't say that she was married. I said that she was dead."

The woman walked back to her stool. She had heard so many inadequate fumblings, sometimes she felt entitled to turn away.

"Holy shit," Maud said, "it's time to get out of here. Do you need something to eat?"

They went to the nearest restaurant, ordered and had a bottle of wine. They talked about their loves. They were important in some way, these old loves of theirs. Remembering them brought the sweetest idealised pleasure and might awaken an interest in a new love.

"You haven't had very long relationships," Frank said, working hard to get his voice between a question and a tease.

"Actually, come to think about it, I haven't had any. One-night stands repeated a few times. Mind you, yours don't seem to have lasted too long either." Maud managed a perfectly pitched laugh.

"But they were meant to."

"And mine weren't? Perhaps you're right. My next big birthday is thirty. I suppose I should soon do something about this. Not yet, definitely not yet."

Frank wondered if it would be too presumptuous to offer himself as a candidate. He decided that it would. This was going to be like walking on glass. He, too, presumed a future.

"I hate my flat. I've been in it too long. It's the same one that I shared with my brother before he met his girlfriend. Much too long. I'd love to buy a house, but can't afford the mortgage on my own."

This was not strictly speaking true, because Maud and Malachy were in the process of selling their parents' house. The emptiness of it had finally got to them.

Frank dithered for only a couple of seconds. "I've recently been thinking the same thing. We could give it a try, don't you think? One with enough rooms to give us both privacy?"

He heard himself. *This is the sensible person that I have not yet become.*

Maud didn't rule it out of hand, immediately. And then wondered why she should. Frank watched the doubts playing on her face. Sometimes saying no too quickly left trails of regret. In this year her dreams had been made up of explosions. A wound had been made on the door of her home. There was little left to protect her. Malachy had Valerie. Maud had a wide-open scar through which all kinds of trouble could break.

And then the secret on top of it all. The burden of it. Her mother had looked for thingamajigs all her life, vague bits of household cutlery and crockery.

"It just goes to show," she would say.

"Show what?"

"It just goes to show," Maud said to Frank.

"Show what?" he asked.

Maud laughed. And then, after the secret, there had been all that other business. She was not sorry that she had followed her nose, she had never had any choice, but it had marked her as a woman. She was a marked woman.

"Well, we could look anyway."

"Great," Frank said, but at the back of his mind he regretted a little, because now he knew that he wasn't going to get the girl. They had created a propriety over which steps had to be counted. Ah well, it was time for a move on.

Maud knew that Malachy would see pitfalls and warn and niggle. She already had him answered: "It's like you and Valerie buying a house. But mine will be a mortgage without sex. And easier to get out of than yours."

Malachy wouldn't like that. She'd better think of something else. The best thing to do sometimes with him was to let him wind out his annoyance, ignore it until it petered out on thin air.

By the time the meal was over, arrangements had been made to go looking. On Sunday.

"That soon?"

"Why not?"

"We're only looking, so far."

* * *

They became experts. They could be in and out in five minutes flat, leaving other viewers peering over and under things. They knew. So far neither of them had felt interested in any house that they had seen. Malachy tutted relief on learning this every Sunday night. Maybe it was just a hobby. And then both Frank and Maud stopped at a kitchen sink and oohed and ahhed a little. They slowed their pace up the stairs. They, too, began to peer over, under and into. They split up and walked to opposite ends of the house, then turned back to meet in the middle. Malachy definitely would not have liked that at all.

"What do you think?"

They got a solicitor who used a disapproving voice. These sorts of arrangements annoyed him. It was like looking down the barrel of a gun. Still, no accounting for tastes. And it wasn't as if either of them was an unpresentable person. Maud and Frank signed on many dotted lines. On the day, Frank wore a Burren tweed jacket, black trousers and a purple shirt. He looked dressed for something big. Maud wore brown jeans, an autumn jacket, a mauve shirt with small buttons and a startling scarf. It changed colour and flow each time she moved. Frank watched it. Maud got chatty about the original deeds. Look, and look.

He had suffered a shock when he had seen her arriving at the solicitor's office, an almost blinding, infuriating shock. He was reduced to the status of a child. He wasn't sure that he could keep his thoughts under wraps. There is nothing worse than reading a face that doesn't respond. He longed to reach out a hand and touch her fingers. Would a simple hand squeeze be allowed, or was she lost to him for ever even before he had found her? She talked to the solicitor about practical things. He undressed her, the scarf from around her neck, the jacket, the shirt. It was excruciating, this waiting for language to change. He wasn't sure if he would be able to carry this civility off. The solicitor was shuffling papers, closing folders. They all three stood up.

Frank asked Maud if she would like a coffee. His voice was thick. "A good strong coffee would help."

"Help what?" Maud said. "Maybe it's a good strong drink we need."

Maud lit a cigarette. The pleasure was written all over her face. Maybe he would take up smoking.

Maud was excited, but not about the same things as him. Her scarf shimmered, taking on new colours like a red-winged blackbird or a peacock winking its tail. He looked at her, careful not to show the awfulness in his head. Just one look and he would let this thing go. For ever.

* * *

They moved in on a Sunday.

"Saturday flit, short sit," Maud said.

Their furniture, from their respective flats, looked meagre. Some of it matched surprisingly well. Other items would have to go; they looked as if they'd dropped from two different lives. Malachy came to help. He behaved like an older brother sending his sister off to the unknown. The work, the heaving, the scrubbing, the lifting, the lining up softened him a little. Funnily enough, he liked Frank. He took out the bottle of red wine, found three large tumbler glasses that had belonged to their parents. He poured, wondering briefly what they would have thought. It shocked him to realise that he didn't know.

They drank to health, strength and happiness. They moved some more furniture. Maud lit a fire. That would be her. Malachy was sad. He poured three more glasses. Maud went in to have a shower.

"Do you want to take yours first?" she asked Frank.

"No, you go first."

Malachy was shocked at the intimacy of the non-intimacy. When she was finished, Frank went into the bathroom.

"Will you be all right?" Malachy asked stiffly. The stiffness came from caring.

"All right? I'll be terrific. I love it."

"No, but I mean, you and Frank and things."

"Things," she laughed. "God, you're a fine old square."

It was years since he had heard her using that word.

"I'll be fine, Malachy. Stop worrying, my dear brother."

Frank rejoined them after his shower, smelling new. Malachy poured the last three glasses, careful not to give himself the last drop. He didn't want bad luck for anyone. Valerie, Caitríona and Marjorie came separately. There was much congratulating and walking from room to room. And more wine. The house was warmed.

Maud slept marvellously, dream free. It was as if she had been here for ever. Frank decided that it would not be a good idea to discuss his dreams. They ate a companionable breakfast, the first of many. Yes, he would be able for this. In no time at all he would be able to have breakfast in his pyjamas.

* * *

They settled in remarkably well. They tiptoed around the unknown domesticities for a short while but soon got used to each other. They would be able to stay out of the way of each other's foibles. He liked to talk at breakfast; she didn't. He liked to switch on the radio first thing in the evening; she didn't. But they both liked to watch bad television once a week. So they chose which programme, which day, and lay in their armchairs. If the phone rang during that time, they didn't answer it. Frank had answered his phone three times during their dinner in the first fortnight. The fourth time Maud said, "This is a dinner table, not a boardroom."

The caller on the other end of the line heard. So they made some ground rules in good faith and good humour.

Maud went on a semi-diet and joined a keep-fit club. On her second evening at the keep-fit club, the woman working the weights beside her fell. She gave out a kind of strangled sigh. Maud and the two other exercisers put down their own weights carefully, as ordered, carefully so as to avoid back injury. The process of keeping fit was fraught with danger. They went over to help the woman get up. What if she was dying? What if the exercise had killed her. Would anyone know the Act of Contrition? Had anyone arrived in time to say it to her parents? Who had arrived first? Why did she not know these things? Had finding the letter diverted her attention from these matters, and had she deliberately welcomed that diversion. Maud left the room as soon as the woman was back on her feet. She forgot to ask for her money back. She went off her semi-diet.

"I think I'll go to body tone instead."

The idea of body tone was to twist, rather than starve, off some of the fat. Each bed had a different rotating part, and this section of the bed moved the various components of the body: hips, waist, buttocks. Legs went up in the air seemingly of their own accord, pushed by fingers of mattress. The women had their hips and leg measurements taken regularly. Maud declined this service. They swapped stories about the way men had left them. One of them admitted that she had also walked out. This admission was not what was needed here. Silence reigned. The machines creaked, swung, threw legs up in the air. Twisted waists. They would waken the following morning regretting opening up those old sores. It would take all of the next day and a night's sleep to recover. Maud buried her face in magazines built around making people want things. 2FM played in the background, trite music, trite comment. Maud decided to get fat if necessary.

Frank and she told stories to each other to fill in time. There was not always a purpose to these stories, but they moved the evenings along.

"Being alone was OK, but we weren't that committed to it. That's why we bought the house together," Maud told Malachy. He was getting used to the whole idea.

If Maud had ever thought that this was second best she never said so. And Frank wouldn't. They took a morning off together and went to breakfast places. They listened out; they were very good eavesdroppers. Men spoke business talk loudly, excited in their agreement on how to make more money for their companies. Their companies, all of which could forget their names in two days flat, if necessary.

"What are you thinking?"

"Nothing much."

"More coffee?"

They went to work together as well, of course. No point in

using two cars. People would start talking. If only there was something to talk about, Frank pined, in his occasional relapses. *I wonder does she ever talk about me to the others in the office? No way, she wouldn't.* He bet she was secretive. Maud noticed that Frank had stopped looking at her like that. Like what? Like that. Like as if he was going to say something more. She also noticed that he had stopped looking at other women like that. Ah well, there you go, maybe it was just a house he had wanted all along.

On Saturday night she watched a talk show on television. The American woman was big. Her thoughts went out on to branches, then she roped them in to create an unattractive picture, a sullen view of the world. She vibrated with the things that needed to be done and said that people could do them. If they wanted to. Big things, big fightbacks. First they had to shake themselves up, look for reasons, not shove everything to the back of the collective mind. Why, in America they let people bomb wherever they wanted as long as none of their soldiers were coming home dead. These and other things could be stopped. Other things like beating up women and children, letting crack into dispensable neighbourhoods, then putting the young men in jail. "We cannot all believe that things are just meant to be." She took a breath. Some men in the audience bristled as one. The women they had married were good looking and mild. They had never known a woman like her, and didn't wish to. Maud longed to have her nerve, to be that alive, to be so free. Frank came in, slightly tipsy, with his stories of the night. The relief of his organised narrative made Maud forget the programme. They watched football, the big European game. It ended in a nil-nil draw. The extra half hour would be played, and if neither side had scored a goal the penalty shoot-out would take place. Frank moved to the fridge to get a beer.

"God, it's a boring game, one and a half hours, another half hour with maybe no score and then the goals. It's like kissing your sister."

Maud decided to go to bed before the final excruciation. Frank was too annoyed with the game to be disappointed.

On Sunday Maud lolled about reading the late edition newspaper. She read the sports page; she wanted to find out about the penalty shoot-out. It was the least she could do for Frank. The newspaper hadn't got it, so she switched on the radio. She'd know the score before he got up. He had a hangover and wandered about the kitchen restlessly, without purpose. It was turning into a makeshift sort of a day.

"Maud, would you like to go somewhere? We could take a drive."

"I'd like to go to my parents' grave."

She had no idea why she had said that. Her voice was steady, almost apathetic.

"OK then, we'll do that."

And so they visited the dead. They drove to her county. Maud grew tense as Frank parked the car. She hadn't brought flowers. He walked behind her, allowing her some moments alone. She never talked about them. Why should she? He had no right to think that she should. By the time he joined her, she was ready to talk about headstones, the preferability of pebbles over flowers, because neither Malachy nor she could guarantee that they would keep it up. But there was a bunch of flowers not quite wilted. Malachy had been here without telling her. She was here without telling him. Maybe it was one of the neighbours. If Maud had been different, Frank could have got his opportunity to hug her. It would have been allowed.

Back in the car she said, "It was a terrible thing. At the funeral I was in shock. I kept thinking, 'This is the worst thing. This is worse than dropping stitches while knitting a diamond patterned jumper.' Then I'd wonder why I was concentrating on such a thing. Anything to stop me thinking about what was really happening. I was afraid to cry. Where exactly are you from?"

There was no danger attached to this allowed intimacy.

"Gearagh, a village. Or I should say a village that was. It's only a ghost now."

"What do you mean?"

"It was drowned to make a dam."

"Holy Jesus. No one ever thinks of that."

"When I was very young, I couldn't have cared less. It was just the past, and I liked our new house. But nearly every time we went for a Sunday drive, my mother would find some excuse to get my father to drive past it. 'Wouldn't it be nice to see what Gearagh looks like in the sun? The rain always makes Gearagh look interesting. The wind is always great on a day like this in Gearagh.'"

And Frank's father would obediently turn the car in the direction of Gearagh. He never said a word. He acted like a man dealing with a wife who had dead children. The car would chug up the hill. Frank and his sister had hated it. Hated his parents and their bloody drowned village. They would get out of the car and stare at the water, his parents seeing streets, and a school with the chalk marks still on the blackboard, and shops, and the two churches, one Protestant, one Catholic, both with their rusting bells. They remembered their house, and the trees planted, and their neighbours, all scattered now. They would talk in hushed whispers as if they had no children to overhear them.

"John Logan went mad, they say."

"He must have gone mad, otherwise how could he have done such a thing?" He was drinking whiskey with a new neighbour in a new village where he had been transported, up to Meath. He had cracked up and hit the neighbour over the head with a slash hook. He thought he was dead, dragged him to the haggard and buried him underneath some straw. The neighbour feigned well. John intended to come back in the morning and do whatever he had to do. When all was quiet, the neighbour raised himself up and crept to the nearest garda station. The guards arrived in the middle of the night and promptly put handcuffs on John. It was lucky for him that the neighbour had lived, otherwise it's more than the mental he would have got.

"Apparently he's out and in England now."

"Holy fuck, they said all this in front of you and your sister?"

"Oh yeah. Standing there seemed to do something to them."

"I'll bet."

Then Frank's parents would bustle the children back into the car as if they'd just been watching budding rhododendrons or rabbits making homes.

"I didn't understand then, but I do now. I was going to dive down, maybe bring them back a picture before they die. But the diving instructor told me that because the water was so full of peat you couldn't see anything. Everything would be too dark. You certainly wouldn't be able to see the chalk on the blackboard through the school window."

He didn't tell Maud about the question mark over his fitness. Just didn't bother, didn't see the point. At teenage time the normal panic between the generations had been skewed for Frank. The usual panic became an awesome worry for Frank's mother. She put everything down to the loss of her village. No wonder he looked deep into the eyes of women.

So Frank had lost his history, too. And in that moment Maud wondered if she could tell him. But would telling him ring a warning bell for her own reputation? Would he think, pedigree, you know, pedigree? Would he believe her?

Maud took her chance. Once she started it was easy. She told it as if it had nothing to do with her, one of their stories that passed the time. Frank pulled the car into a picnic spot.

"When I went into the gallows room in Mountjoy, the hang house if you will, I knew that I had gone so far that I was going to have to go further. It was like as if I had always known that men had been hanged, and vaguely supposed that the odd one might not have done it, but now I really knew. I had visited the spot. I had realised. The truth leaves a resonance. And then that took me the first time to America. I think I meant to go further than I did that time, but I lost my nerve. And then I went back. And I think I will go one more time. I wasn't always this obsessional, although really I don't think of it as obsessional. I think of it as a considered response. Do you understand?"

"I think I do. Things happen and have impossible unknown effects. Immigrants to southern California used straw and Scottish broom to pack their belongings, so Scottish broom now grows wild in countries where it should not be at all. Firemen fighting bush fires go up in flames all the time, because the thing has a lot of oil in it, the stems are thin and the space between them allows the air to create a big fire. They shoot into flames."

"I don't see what that's got to do with anything."

"I do," Frank said.

"Well, I'm glad you see something. I'm afraid to tell people. It's not like finding out that you have had a poet in the family."

They both laughed, big thundering things of relief. Frank drove the car back on to the road.

"One thing though," he said, "you'll have to tell Malachy."

CHAPTER 26

MALACHY AND VALERIE set a date. It was hard to say who asked who. They toasted each other. And the future. They left the restaurant, flushed. They were relieved that their lives had been shunted forward a little. It was bad to stand still, and long engagements could spin themselves out. The lack of declaration could leave more room to manoeuvre than people could handle. The organisation of the wedding would tell both of them new things about each other.

"Who should we invite?"

Malachy discovered that Valerie held old grudges. There were people who were definitely not coming. He said that you couldn't ask one set of a family and not the other. She said that you could do what you bloody well liked for your own wedding. All staff members, from both their schools, would have to be asked. Yes, different schools. Valerie had studied more and moved to secondary level. She had been afraid that spending all day together at work might have eventually driven them mad. Malachy had stayed where he was, promotion having promised more promotion.

They went through the lists. They did Valerie's first. John, the big tall woodwork teacher, who wore a hint of sleaze as if it was a badge of honour. He had a wife, sometimes spoke about her in a deprecating way. He never used her first name. It would be interesting to see how she measured up to his comments. It would definitely be possible for the others to gauge that over a long day's revelry. Not Malachy and Valerie, they would be too busy. Vincent, geography, who clapped his hands together continuously. Sometimes it got on people's nerves. But there were too many good things about him to allow the annoyance to last. He went ballroom dancing at weekends. He had no embarrassment about this, but the women could see that the other men had. Philip, history, who had not been born in Ireland. He radiated total contentment, and gratitude that his life had turned out so good. He took his wife out for dinner once a week. She had told him that this was required, and he believed her. Lawrence, art. Rangy and appeared to be shy. Which was a way of getting the women to like him more. Maybe unintentional. If any of them had cottoned on to him, they never said. He had strings of ex-girl-friends; no one believed that any of them had ever fallen out of love with him. He was one of the reasons that Valerie should not let her engagement wear itself thin. Clodagh, Irish. She complained loudly about the men in her life who had all let her down. It never struck her that her colleagues might wonder about such severe serial bad luck. Her trust in their loyalty was refreshing. Madonna, mathematics, who wore her name proudly. Its time would come around. She wore yellow a lot and could take or leave people, it was all the same to her. But she got hooked on small problems as if they were part of her subject. The other teachers humoured her. The new young teacher, just out of college — what was her name? — English, who drove them all nuts, hanging on to their adult lines as if she had a right. But she couldn't be left out. And lastly June, French. She believed that her calling was worth more than all the others put together. Miss Notice Box, using phrases that the others couldn't understand in an accent that was uncalled for in a school staff room. Who was she trying to impress? This wasn't the south of France. She wore clothes designed to show every contour on her body. She threw it around shamelessly, stretching and sighing out loud at every opportunity, leaving all and nothing to the imagination. Valerie hated her. Hated the blatantness of her body talk. She shouldn't have worried. Malachy found it too obvious to be attractive, the times that he had met her at Valerie's school dos. And then she would smile at the women, trying to get them back on her side. She might need them sometime. Yes, Valerie hated her. And then she had a horrible laugh, one that tried not to act her age. Valerie really hated her. But she would have to be asked.

It was easier now. Colleagues were done, relations were written out on one sheet of paper. Now they could move on to friends. People they wanted to be there. But here, too, there were problems. Malachy could not remember what old girl-friends he had confessed to, so he wasn't sure who to risk mentioning. Valerie waited to pounce. For his part he remembered painfully each and every name that had been part of her past. But he didn't pounce. He ignored his breath lapses and waited for the ache to pass over.

Eventually it was all done, a minefield negotiated. Now there was the hotel, the music, the cake, the flowers. But what about the bridesmaid? Valerie wanted, and didn't want, Maud. She wanted her because of Malachy. But she herself didn't want her to be so near on the day. Malachy wanted her and that was that. Neither of them said anything yet. They would leave the last nettle until later. They went to bed. Malachy watched Valerie sleep. It was strange the way a person's colour changed, as if they were dead for a while. He curled up beside her, overcome with thoughts of his luck. He hadn't yet tried out the sound of the word wife. Maybe tonight was a good time to do it. When she wasn't looking and couldn't see him stumble. *Come here to me. Bring over your dreams behind me.*

Valerie woke in the morning and said, "We forgot about bridesmaids." Plural made it easier. "We'll ask Maud."

"Of course," said Malachy. As if they would ever have done anything else.

The invitations were sent out in the post all at the same time, so that no one would have to wait for days to see if they had been left out.

In their arguments they discovered even more joy than they had known. Not in the disagreements themselves, which were occasionally fraught, but in the fact that they could disagree, paddle out almost to the furthest point of hurt, but fight their way back to safe ground. The fact that they were not made nervous by dissension, and yet didn't create it for its own sake, and the fact that the gloves were kept on. They assumed familiarity in argument, assumption based on real fact.

The pre-wedding nights for going out were appointed. Maud didn't really like it, these nights, Valerie with her workmates, Malachy with his, Valerie with women, Malachy with men. It made an American wake out of it all. Or elevated the marriage into such a restricted place that it was frightening. This is the last time you will see me before I marry. So we mark it because I will never be the same again. You're not mine any more. What balderdash. Malachy didn't want the marriage to matter that much to Maud. He didn't care about anyone else, but he didn't like drastic changes between his twin and himself. Some changes, yes, ones that they made between themselves involving bits of hurt that could be healed later. He hung back from too much banner waving about the wedding even though that was difficult, marked him as a malingerer, because the thing had gathered a noise of its own. A height from which someone could be pushed.

* * *

They grouped around the bar table, all of them out tonight. And then the moment happened. The turning point that might destroy everything.

"Stop hogging Malachy."

But it was her last chance. And what a place to play it out. But she didn't do this maliciously, no matter how it seemed. Those were not her intentions. She had been afraid. She moved her body slightly forward, blocking a small part of the crowd.

"There's something I have to tell you."

Frank heard the sentence as if it had been screamed out. He had mixed emotions, annoyance and loyalty. The latter was strongest, and he proceeded to draw everyone closer to him, his heart dropping at the thought that he would need every story he had ever known. And he'd have to tell them so well, better than his capabilities, in order to keep them occupied, away from Maud's revelations.

"Remember the day we went home — sorry, to our parents' house — after the funeral?"

"Home will do," Malachy said testily, wary of Maud's tone of voice, sensing an unpleasant revelation.

"Well, I found this letter."

The trouble is, Frank thought, *the truest cliché of them all is that there are two ways of looking at everything. And two ways of feeling about things.* He no longer lusted after Maud, or so he told himself. At least, less often. He could now manage normal household patterns, look at her, smile at her. Look directly at her without revealing everything, without thinking, *Hold it there. Let's stare each other out as if it was a game, during which something might happen.*

There were still difficult times, having a drink in her company. Couldn't he just veer too far in one direction of their conversation? They did talk in sentences that had innuendo. Couldn't he overstep the mark and watch carefully how she reacted, push a little further, drink less than her? My God, what was he thinking? A new variation of getting a woman when she's drunk? But couldn't he try it a little and blame the atmosphere afterwards? But would it destroy their delicate days?

Then there was the difficult time of after having a drink. The next day, when he felt a little cold and longed to casually lean over the table, put his hand on hers and say, "We need a nap." Nothing more. And the difficult time when they weren't drinking at all. When reasonable satisfied logic demanded that he say something clearly. He had no nerve. You couldn't say that about Maud.

She continued her conversation with Malachy. As yet, it couldn't really be called that, it was all one way. Malachy was staring at her, saying very little, an occasional, "Go on." They were both oblivious to their surroundings. Her body was now further forward, blocking a complete half vision of the crowd. What other stories did Frank have? Let's see, he was no good at jokes.

"You told me that before," Malachy said to Maud, his voice cold.

"Some things have to be repeated. Surely you of all people should know that," Maud said.

"OK, go on."

The fact that Frank had his emotions under control made life generally a lot easier. He reacted to other people in a more or less balanced way. His work was less stressful. The truth was, and he now admitted it freely, he had been angling for Maud since first seeing her. That time in the canteen, her face all animated, her gestures full of life. He remembered thinking where the hell had she come from. And it had affected everything. Particularly how he saw his colleagues, because, in all honesty, he had been continuously watching to see how she was getting on with other men. Well, was the answer. Always smiling, or looking serious, or looking some damn way. And it had almost driven him mad. Now that they were friends, he found it much easier to cope. He did not put her image in bed with every other man. *Bloody friends!* Only one thing would make it easier still, if she would just say one sentence that would single him out, above all others. If first himself could understand that he was special, and then if the others could be made to understand it, too. But even he knew that this was unreasonable. Because if he got that sentence, he would want another. And want that one repeated. And another one. And it repeated often. That's what love is, repeated sentences. All this time he knew he'd have to come up with another story once the present anecdote was over.

"You were doing this, you did this, this whatever you call it, because of shock. You're holding on to connections, that's all. I know I should have seen more of you. Drop it now, now that we have spoken. We don't have to think about him. I know it's a shock, and all that, but we really don't have to think about him," Malachy said.

"Some knowledge demands reaction," Maud said.

"Baloney. Where did you hear that?"

It was a tactic he often used, intimating that Maud could not think things of her own.

Frank told another work conference story. What had actually happened was that a woman was giving a paper when the arrival of the MEP, the big man, was announced. The paper had to be stopped, mid-sentence. A handful of men, and one woman, ran out to have their pictures taken with him. The MEP. All the rest of the women and a few men stayed in the room. There weren't many men at the conference; it was a women's thing, poverty and crime. While the cameras were clicking outside and shrewd one-liners were being frisbeed out to produce smiles on faces, the women sat quietly waiting for the big man, the MEP, to come in. They didn't even speak to each other. It was as if these minutes weren't happening. The woman's paper had to be abandoned when the big man did come in. Frank was trying to tell the big man's jokes and a bit of gossip about him, nothing too daring. But it was the picture of the silent women that kept intruding on his verbiage. His story was being ruined. He would lose his audience.

Malachy was shouting at Maud. By now her body was totally blocking out the sight of everyone. He was shouting at her as if she was a child and he an adult. It's strange the way adults shout at children, but when the children get older and could bear it, or shout back, the adults lower the tone. The prison warder in Mountjoy had told Maud about that barrister she mentioned. He was very young when he was in first. Political, all that family political, from the granny down. One warder used to scream abuse at him, just to show that he wasn't showing him favouritism because of his age. That was the signal for Sean to run up and find the chocolates that the warder had just put under the pillow. Must have been nearly the same age as a son of his own. Now what was Frank at? If he didn't assemble his thoughts better, keep this night going, the whole thing would be out in the open. Here and now. And Malachy wouldn't like that. Neither would Maud. Not until she was ready.

Caitríona and Majorie were here, too. They were all here, ghosts and all. *I wonder how far Maud is with the story now?* Majorie was still going out with the man she had met at Reynard's. She was talking about him now. Frank could take a breather. She was fond of the man, she said. She was busy forgiving him one night for an ex-lover when the woman walked in. The woman took her jumper off over her head, directly in front of them. The way she did it made Marjorie crawl. It turned her off her forgiving for the night. And then she met her in the toilet. She thought she'd never get out of there. Frank overheard. They wouldn't have wanted that, this was women's talk. He sympathised to himself. *You should be careful there, Marjorie. I'd watch that if I were you.*

By now Maud and Malachy were facing each other, their eyes spitting. No one would have dared interrupt them. Not even Valerie. She hid her annoyance well. *Typical! Tonight of all nights.* Hadn't they got enough of each other. Would it never end. And yet she had to admit that him being a twin had probably made him into the kind of man he was, so she supposed she would have to put up with it. *Thank Christ they aren't identical,* she thought.

"To recap," Maud said.

"Oh shut up. What do you mean to recap? What do you think this is, a trial?"

"No, perhaps it's a classroom and I'm trying to get the salient points remembered."

You have to admire her, Frank thought.

"A penny for them, Frank? You look a troubled man," Majorie said. If those two didn't keep their voices down, even if they did, come to think of it, the others would hear. They were already getting curious. The titillation of loud whispers could get too much. Frank willed them to keep their voices down. It worked for a few minutes.

"My parents. . ."

"You mean our parents."

Certainly, interruption would have to be postponed. Maud's bag had been stolen from her car, rifled, then dropped into the nearest rubbish bin. It was Frank who had helped her, he who had rummaged through all that shit to see if he could find her father's pipe. Him. Not Malachy. He had found it. And Maud had given him a grateful hug. Well, you wouldn't really call it a hug. It was more a frontal pat, using her arms instead of a hand.

"It was a complicated smell: body powders, sweat, sorrow, regret."

She had used that description when talking to Frank. He supposed she did remember it like that, so couldn't change it for Malachy. She was definitely in America by now. He wondered what Malachy would make of that.

"Why America?"

"Because that's. . ." Frank couldn't hear the rest. He was still trying to talk to the others and to eavesdrop at the same time.

"I don't see why you had to pick America. If you travel far enough west, you'll end up in the east. The world is round, you know," Malachy said.

"Yes, sir," Maud said. It was an odd thing for Maud to be using Malachy's job against him.

"Why are you doing this to me?" Malachy wheedled.

"I'm not doing anything to you. I didn't do anything against you. It's just that if I am going to offend I want to do it with authenticity. And I will offend, when I take on the next stage. I think we should look for a posthumous pardon."

That's my girl, thought Frank, *stand up to him*.

"We! We! You must be bloody joking," Malachy hissed,

then said, in a defeated sort of voice, "Why do you want to do it?"

"For the principle. Does no one have any of those things any more?"

"There is a difference between a reason and an excuse, I suppose. But if you are prepared to make yourself into a political person, that sort of one, look what it will do to you. You will be on the outside for ever. I doubt if you'll see much more promotion."

"Fuck the promotion. There's more to life than promotion."

Malachy winced.

"Do you think we were born to . . ."

At least the conversation seemed to be degenerating into ordinary insults.

"But in the case of *our* murder . . ."

"What do you mean *our* murder? Keep your voice down, for Christ's sake."

Malachy grabbed Maud by the arm and pulled her upwards. His intentions were to get her out the door. Frank tried to hide the kerfuffle. Maud tightened her heart into a thin smile. Frank supposed that it was a mark of some extraordinary thing that she could forgive Malachy such bad manners. And then he intervened. In a venomous whisper he said, "Would the two of you stop, please. This instant. Now. Immediately."

And they did, both glowering at each other.

"Now, whose round is it? Or are we going into a kitty now?"

CHAPTER 27

MALACHY SPENT A long night with Maud, less because he wanted to than because he needed to question her. She told him a lot of what she had done since finding the letter. She left some things out, Gerard for one. He would have been a diversion. Malachy would have wished that she had concentrated on him alone. He had to get away for the next day. It was hard to lie to Valerie, and not a thing he wanted to cultivate within himself, but he needed a morning out in the open. He was going to marry Valerie, they would vex each other on a daily basis, but this was more than a simple thing to vex over.

He went to a quiet spot in the Phoenix Park. It was an overcast day, and although the trees were full of leaves that made rustling noises when they rubbed up against each other, he took no comfort from his surroundings. He kicked stones.

There were two things: their uncle, their granduncle for God's sake, and this American nonsense. It was closure, that's all. He'd heard talk about that. It was that all right. The word would not have been around in his uncle's time. It was odd to think now of that thing that he had seen on television. A man had watched a woman lying blindfolded on the gurney for fifteen minutes while they waited for the governor's call. (Was he not at his desk? Had he slept in? Did his working breakfast run over?) And when the noise in the room changed, the man had said, "Something's happening," and then he addressed the gurney: "Take her away, she's all yours."

He had explained this to the cameras outside. Malachy had accidentally seen it. He hadn't slept well that night, but he had put it out of his head next morning. Under no circumstances was he going to discuss that sort of thing. With anybody. On that sort of day where did the relatives stay? Where had his relatives stayed? It would be the emptiest of nights. Was there a sense of pity? Imagine knowing that you would never see the sea again. But that would come to us all. How had his relatives coped, coming to Dublin from a place where they knew all the bends in the road? He hoped that they had had a friendly hotel. All those years without knowing that people had been talking about the tunes played that night. The thought of it would put years on a person. Those Americans, the ones who wanted to watch, were they served refreshments? Those Americans in the pens that Maud had insisted on describing, the look of the man that had bored into her, that she would never, ever forget. Those Americans. Did they ever wake up and forget where they were?

See, he was at it now, too. That's what Maud had done, her and her meddling. She had brought up hurt that he never knew was there, and he would have been happy to remain ignorant. He did not have to know everything. Why couldn't she have left it alone?

And his uncle? What if he was guilty? What if he had an uncle who was a murderer? Well, he supposed he'd just have to say that it had nothing to do with him. In a way Malachy felt that it would be easier to think of him as guilty. But according to Maud, and she certainly seemed to have done her home-work, this was not the case. She had done a brave thing, he supposed, but foolhardy and unnecessary, of course. Always the same. He tried to remember things in their childhood that pointed to this day, but he couldn't. Not a single thing. He remembered that every time an old gray-haired priest came to their house their mother batted the cushions and hissed him-self and Maud out to play. What was all that about? Oh, the curse of this, he couldn't start examining every single bloody thing. He kicked some more stones and made his way back to his car. What he hated most about Maud at the moment was that she was right. But he wasn't going to be right with her. He would have to pull away from her. Because now she wanted to get in touch with some TDs. To start the process of a pardon. Suffering Jesus, did she not know what publicity that would take down on their heads. Yes, of course, he would have to deal in some way with the uncle thing, but as briefly as possible, and he was not going to be Pied Pipered down some crazy road of Maud's because of it.

And if it was true that his main worry was that Valerie might not marry him if she knew, then maybe he wouldn't tell her. He hadn't got this near his wedding to have Maud and some dead relative blow the whole thing to pieces.

CHAPTER 28

THAT NIGHT MALACHY looked at Valerie as she slept. It frightened him. What if she couldn't love him any more? If the world was fair, he would be contemplating what if he fell out of love with her. That's what people about to be married were supposed to think. What if they didn't want to make love any more? If one day it just got too ridiculous, too personal, too incestuous. Would they be able to weather that, with everybody else boasting about how many times they did it. It's a terrible responsibility to say that you would want to bonk someone for ever. That's what he should have been thinking about, but instead he was thinking about the bedlam in his own history. It would have been good to have been able to weep, to cry.

Two nights before the wedding he thought he'd better do

it. It was not, after all, possible to leave it untold. If he left it until the night before and Valerie wanted to cancel, it would leave things even worse than worse. This way they could stop the circus from leaving home ground, ring around the country and say, "Don't bother coming to Dublin, it's all off." Whose job would that be? His or the groomsman's? Not Valerie's, because the fiasco wouldn't be her fault. He would have to do it now anyway because they would not be staying together tomorrow night. They had better keep some old custom, in the hope that even a little nod to the old-fashioned might bring them luck. He made a lot of noise, shifting about from one side of the chair to the other. He spent a lot of time talking about the ingredients in the dinner they had just eaten.

But when he started to tell her it became remarkably easy, like reading poetry at school, which always surprised him. He took a run at the story, allowing Valerie's odd exclamation only enough time to breathe before he hurtled on. He discovered, in the telling, that this American thing of Maud's was useful. It shifted the balance from their own mud. And it was also more interesting, that it was still being done in this day and age, the trimmings of cruelty and barbarity surrounding it. It saved him from coasting his own past and testing it against the present.

When Malachy was finished he waited nervously, as if he had just done an oral examination.

"I knew that there was something up with her," Valerie said.

"But not that?" Malachy said.

"Not that. How could I have guessed that? But something serious."

"How? When?"

"On that day. She came down from upstairs very pale and made a huge deal about finicky things. I suspected that she had found something. One would expect that."

"Well, what do you think?"

"About what?"

"About us."

"What has it got to do with us?"

"It doesn't change anything?"

"Like what?"

"Like us."

"Oh, for God's sake, you didn't think that, you poor thing? But it does give me a lot of advantage points."

She was laughing. She was actually laughing. He would now have to pretend that he had never been worried.

"I always knew that there was something peculiar about the American holidays. Not enough photos. Not enough tittle-tattle. But I had it down to an affair with a married man," Valerie said, getting up to make coffee, pushing her hair back off her face in a way that he now knew had become familiar.

"You don't think that she did it on purpose?"

"Disturb the sleeping dog, you mean?"

"Yes."

It was important for him that Valerie wouldn't think this.

"Of course not. And I know that you'll always have to defend her, no matter what she does. But some people cannot patch over things. It's like returning corpses. Aborigines always want them back. Some things have to be brought home."

* * *

At Maud and Frank's house things were a little more edgy. Maud wondered what was going on over at Malachy's and flustered herself enormously about the kitchen, trying to fill her mind until the telephone would ring. And he would get in touch, as soon as a moment fell between his dual responsibilities, because he would know that she was waiting. Frank watched her bending over. He reprimanded himself for his coarseness. And the return of longing that he thought he had beaten. Maybe after the wedding there would be less competition from Malachy, leaving some possibility for him. Certainly during the honeymoon.

CHAPTER 29

THE NIGHT BEFORE Malachy and Valerie married, there was a frost on the ground. It was a windless, hushed dusk that made nightwalkers in the country think of solitude. Sounds would carry across a field on a night like this.

* * *

The guests gathered, converging like shafts of stars on the spot. They parked cars, women got out daintily from the carefully washed vehicles, husbands told their wives that they liked that perfume. People going out together for a long time wondered what they should do, wondered if they were leaving it too late and tried to detach themselves from the sentiment of the moment. New couples tried nonchalance. Not all of them succeeded. People thought of old lovers and were ashamed.

Unhappy single people thought of how they hated weddings; happy single people prepared to enjoy themselves thoroughly, at everyone else's expense, if needs be.

Malachy jittered mercilessly. This was no joke. The best man tried to calm him. The best man was Frank. At the last moment, while trawling through his lists of friends, it had seemed the most compact thing to do. The organ music began to play. Malachy had dithered about the hotel music. Should he keep the fiddle in, the one that Maud had suggested? Should he throw it out? It stayed. Malachy turned to watch Valerie walking up the aisle. He should be allowed to do that.

Malachy found it impossible to know what he was thinking during the ceremony. And he wanted to know. He wanted to be able to remember. This was a place for the genuine. Valerie's voice sounded stronger than normal, certain, absolutely certain. Only for one moment had she thought, *I don't mean a word of this*. It was come hell or high water time. She looked at Malachy, as if staring into the sea.

Photographs were taken. The sun performed. There was a crater, not remarked upon today, so far, where Malachy's parents should have been. But when Maud squeezed his hand, he knew what she was saying to him. How had this sister of his, who was supposed to retain a good measure of nervousness, become so strong?

She whispered at the side of his face, "It's hard keeping up with bad news. Don't think of anything bad, not today."

Whatever on earth had his sister become?

At the hotel the day took on its own momentum. Food was eaten, drink was drunk, jokes were told, old stories were aired, speeches and the hard references to missing people were got over. The women came and went to the toilet. There was a lot of looking at the bride's dress, the hair of the bridesmaids, the flowers. Such talking. The dance floor was cleared. No one noticed the fiddle.

CHAPTER 30

I T WAS WHILE the honeymoon was taking place that Maud made final arrangements about her decision. One last time to America. The honeymoon meant two fewer people to raise eyebrows. And maybe argue. And try to back her into a spot. Niggle her, harass her, drive her mad. Ostracise her, label her, give her no choice but to scream at them. This way there was only Frank, and he wouldn't dare.

Now she was sorry she had told him, not because of the telling itself, but because he might question her. And she did not want that, did not want the assumption of familiarity. His niece, Ailish, was staying, had been for a number of weeks now. She was a cross between a precocious young adult and a child still. Her belief in the equality of her meagre experience, her eternal wide-eyed questions could be grating on the nerves.

She was manageable though, not too aggravating. And mostly she was bearable. Except that she didn't go to bed early enough. She would be useful now, though, would divert Frank. He wouldn't have the opportunity to ask direct questions. He certainly didn't have the right to corner Maud, which is what he would have to do if he wanted to extract information from her. Frank noticed that Maud was getting very chatty with his niece. He knew exactly what she was doing. Well, let her go, he had his own secrets. Wasn't he from a drowned village? Two could play at that game. He'd make something of his past yet. With him, disappointment always sprouted pettiness.

CHAPTER 31

IN NEW YORK, Maud almost succumbed to fatigue. But this was the last lap. This travelling, with such purpose, was unsettling the principle of her homeliness. She was tired of fighting with timetables. But she had a job to do. There is a bell in Kyungju, Korea. A monk was trying for the right sound, but it wouldn't come. No matter how he boiled the copper, it didn't sound right. He knew that what was needed was a baby. So, for the sake of the sound of a bell, a mother sacrificed her child. The bell still rings loud and clear, "Emmile". Emmy for Mammy, the sound of the baby still calls. It is treasure number one in Korea. Abraham almost did the same thing. Maud wouldn't sacrifice a son, if she had one. Not even if it forgave all evil. And what was evil? Before the arrival and greeting of sin into her own life, she had thought that they were the same thing. The monk had a job to do. So had she. She had her own symbol to make.

Maud telephoned Gerard because he was the only person she knew in this city. He was a glorious thought because of that. He came to her hotel and still didn't ask too many questions. He was dropping out of his real life, of which she knew nothing, in order to drink with her, tease some intimacy into the open, trade as little or as much as was needed. They went to the bedroom, took off their clothes and did what she once believed to be a sin. How marvelous to have left all that. The leaving had been the greatest gift of all.

In old family photographs she looked cold. They were taken before sin. Always in the summer. She had no photographs taken since she knew. Before is a place. Before I knew. To know is to have something given to you, like a ball in a game. It's up to the player to do what they can or will with it. Knowing about her uncle had put a thick heavy feel to her life, as if a loss was leaning on her. Words from the dead had become audible. Seeing the news from Delaware. It wasn't seeing that created problems for Maud, it was feeling. Seeing is merely about reflection on the retina. Maud had seen fishing in the distance, quiet men sitting at the river on the edge of the town, staring into the water, some of them puffing smoke. And she hadn't bothered to go close enough to find out that fish do not lie down peacefully on the bank and just die. She certainly hadn't wanted to see, or feel, the flailing about in the unaccustomed air.

Gerard made love so carefully that Maud almost talked to him. But nothing gave in her. She didn't become broken.

* * *

Five hours ahead, Frank made every effort to stay busy. He was aggravated beyond belief. He had to keep working diligently. He shifted a long intractable problem from his desk. His superiors were pleased with him. He knew that Maud was up to something. He was infuriated, so he solved another desk problem. If his father ever walked into the room when Frank was young and being utterly unruly, bad mannered, thick as two short planks, his father froze and backed out. It was best to leave that kind of thing to the mother. Frank followed her emotional bribery out of rage into the satisfied light of manners and civility. And if he had followed her, he could follow Maud, too. And could surely make her catch up with him, as they formed a circle of pursuit. He, too, had been told terrifying stories, about drowning. He was scared thinking about these things. And furious because of that. More problems at work were solved.

* * *

Maud and Gerard turned out of sleep to each other again. She heard a sound like the distant voice of a loved one. But how could she hear that? She'd never had a loved one. She thought of Frank and was shocked. He came into her head like the winter light in a movie.

Afterwards, Maud and Gerard talked a little. It seemed the mannerly thing to do, because he knew and she knew that they would not see each other again.

"I'm going to France on my holidays next year," she said.

"Well, I'm going to Mexico," he replied. "Maud, do you realise that sometimes the most important thing to know is not to know?"

Sometimes the most unlikely people say things that mean nothing to them.

"Oh, for Christ's sake," Maud said, wishing that he'd get to hell out of this room and give her time to have her regret in private. They did exchange a kiss at the door of her hotel room. But although on the lips, it was formal.

It took Maud five days to do her tasks. The very brazenness of it might take the focus off her, a stranger in this land.

After tomorrow she would leave America for ever. Not the place. She might come back and see other things. But she would leave this America. She had not unpacked all her belongings. She fiddled with the toiletries that were on her dressing table. They were wonderfully familiar.

* * *

The news items in the United States said that, mysteriously, a model of an electric chair had been found in the grounds of the White House at dawn. The groundsman who found it said that it was eerie, sitting there like that, all straight. There was a note pinned to it. It said, "All Your Signatures Have Come Home to Roost." Handwriting experts were examining it. Leads would be followed. The medium sized model was small enough to have been transported in a large suitcase. Some people had seen a woman wheeling a case in the area, but she had been discounted. Enquiries had been made with a Mr Gerard Lethard, whose telephone number was found on the street opposite the spot where the chair had been positioned, but Mr Lethard had no connection with Washington and was as puzzled as the officers who had called on him. He was a PR man for a record company. The CEO of the company was

interviewed and tried not to look too delighted with the exposure. Handwriting experts were also examining that note. The
model was extraordinarily accurate and detailed. Figurative art
almost. Somebody had to have made the thing. Leads would
be followed. An advertising company was floating the idea of
conceptualising whatever there was to conceptualise. They
could always back off if it didn't appear to be a runner. It was
a mystery how the man or men who did this had managed to
breach the fence. Courtesy of the recently beamed Sky News,
Frank saw the clips. Malachy was still on his honeymoon.

On an arts programme on public television, critics discussed the meaning of the chair: "Other than the obvious, of
course . . ."

A prison officer on a death row had let slip that they had
all been on high alert for the last two days. Apparently letters
had arrived addressed to every single man and woman on
death row. Each had contained a single tablet which turned
out to be harmless aspirin. But chaos had been created and all
leave suspended. It had cost millions of dollars. Then a post-
card arrived addressed to all the state and prison governors saying, "So what if it had been poison? You are going to do it
anyway."

"It's all of a piece," the art critic said. But the other panel-
list claimed it for drama, the stage, the timing of the letters. It
was all timing.

"All of a piece, as I said."

* * *

The Customs men didn't even notice Maud as she walked past
them. There were no Special Branch men to stop her. No one

was watching her, except Frank. Ailish was there, too, inter-
rupting his curiosity. It gave Maud time to hide from it. But
at home, as the evening wore on, Maud felt warm sympathy
for Frank. She had at least hit back at her history. What could
he do, build a village so high up a mountain that no one could
reach it? She also remembered the way he had swaggered con-
fidently into her thoughts in New York. So later, with the grass
whispering to itself and the wind howling outside, as if it had
all the space of a country setting in which to caper about,
Maud and Frank went to bed together. They got on with the
vernacular of the night.

KITTY FITZGERALD

"Mystery and politics, a forbidden sexual attraction that turns into romance; Kitty Fitzgerald takes the reader on a gripping roller coaster through the recent past. In *Small Acts of Treachery* a woman of courage defies the power not only of the secret state but of sinister global elites. This is a story you can't stop reading, with an undertow which will give you cause to reflect." Sheila Rowbotham

"[*Small Acts of Treachery*] is a super book with a fascinating story and great characters. The book is all the more impressive because of the very sinister feeling I was left with that it is all too frighteningly possible." *Books Ireland*

ISBN 086322 297 8; Paperback

"*Snapdragons* is a rattling one-sit read, rich with Irish rhythms and laced with a wonderfully bitter and witty ongoing dialogue between the heroine Bernice and her cantankerous, wheedling God. The early, Irish part of the novel is a powerful evocation of a godfearing rural community which reveals itself to be every bit as cruel as the seedy Birmingham underworld to which the girls escape." *Northern Review*

"Startling, humorous, light of touch." *Books Ireland*

ISBN 0 86322 258 7; Paperback

"Marie McGann is a real find. She writes with the exhilaration and defiance of youth and the wisdom of age. A moving and triumphant novel." *Fay Weldon*

"An assured debut . . . At its heart [it] is about love in its many forms, and the struggle to throw off the shackles of defensiveness and self preservation and at last attain the freedom to love without fear." *Sunday Tribune*

ISBN 0 86322 271 4; Paperback

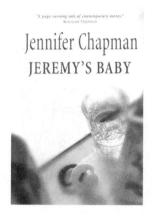

"Anything Jennifer Chapman writes must be taken seriously." *The Times*

"Set against a backdrop of Aga cookery, weekend lunches in the country, arts review programmes on television, it's also a novel about birth and death, love and jealousy, friendship and betrayal . . . But it's in the development of the characters, and in the author's near-scientific fascination with the workings of their minds, that the book's strength lies." *Sunday Tribune*

ISBN 0 86322 277 3; Paperback

ROSEMARY CONRY
Flowers of the Fairest

"Has the ring of authenticity. This is a book to be recommended. . .
Surprisingly, the story is told with much humour." *Irish Independent*

"A fascinating first-hand account of one child's experience of TB in the
1940s. It is full of interesting details of the little everyday routines of life
on a veranda, with all its pain and its fun. . . A lovely book that gives us
a fascinating insight into a world that thankfully we will never know."
Books Ireland

ISBN 0 86322 303 6; Paperback

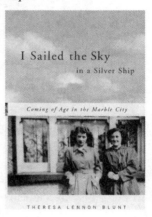

THERESA LENNON BLUNT
I Sailed the Sky in a Silver Ship

"Much more than a chronicle of life in Ireland, it is the story of a girl
desperate to escape the misery and embarrassment . . . The author's
descriptive powers vividly evoke her time and place, and she has
succeeded in relating her tale of a turbulent childhood and youth with
little trace of self-pity." *BookView Ireland*

"From the opening passages of the book the reader is swept back in time
and place through the author's descriptive powers, rich narrative, and
exquisite use of metaphor." *The Harp*

ISBN 0 86322 304 4; Paperback

MARY ROSE CALLAGHAN
The Visitors' Book

"Callaghan takes the romantic visions some Americans have of Ireland
and dismantles them with great comic effect. . . It is near impossible not
to find some enjoyment in this book, due to the fully-formed character of
Peggy who, with her contrasting vulnerability and searing sarcasm,
commands and exerts an irresistible charm." *Sunday Tribune*

ISBN 0 86322 280 3; Paperback

ELIZABETH WASSELL
The Thing He Loves

"A very fine novel: intriguing, dynamic and heartfelt." Colum McCann

"An intriguing and unsettling novel, mainly due to its preoccupation with
the darkness present in human nature. In Gabriel Phillips she has created
a character that could have stepped out of the pages of any Bret Easton
Ellis novel." *Sunday Tribune*

ISBN 0 86322 290 0; Paperback

WILSON JOHN HAIRE
The Yard

"This riproaring yarn about a lad plucked from a rural Belfast environment and plonked into the Harland & Wolff shipyard as an office boy has enough meat in it to service perhaps a dozen books of memoirs, but the author, whose thinly-disguised autobiography it is, has compressed them all into a smorgasbord of earthy irreverence, hardnosed stoicism and some of the most ribtickling anecdotes we've heard this side of Frank McCourt." *Books Ireland*

ISBN 0 86322 296 X; Paperback

JOHN B. KEANE
The Bodhrán Makers

The first and best novel from one of Ireland's best-loved writers, a moving and telling portrayal of a rural community in the '50s, a poverty-stricken people who never lost their dignity.

"Furious, raging, passionate and very, very funny." *Boston Globe*

"This powerful and poignant novel provides John B. Keane with a passport to the highest levels of Irish literature." *Irish Press*

"Sly, funny, heart-rending. . . Keane writes lyrically; recommended."
Library Journal

ISBN 0 86322 300 1; Paperback

KEN BRUEN

"Bleak, amoral and disturbing, *The Guards* breaks new ground in the Irish thriller genre, replacing furious fantasy action with acute observation of human frailty." *Irish Independent*

"Both a tautly written contemporary *noir* with vividly drawn characters and a cracking story, *The Guards* is an acute and compassionate study of rage and loneliness . . . With Jack Taylor, Bruen has created a true original." *Sunday Tribune*

ISBN 0 86322 281 1; Paperback

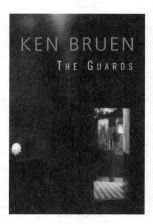 

"Jack Taylor is back in town, weighed down with wisecracks and cocaine . . . Somebody is murdering young male travellers and Taylor, with his reputation as an outsider, is the man they want to get to the root of things . . . Compulsive . . . rapid fire . . . entertaining." *Sunday Tribune*

"Upholds his reputation for edgy, intelligent, thriller noirs." *Ri-Ra*

ISBN 0 86322 294 3; Paperback

KEN BRUEN
The Magdalen Martyrs

The third Jack Taylor from one of the most innovative, exciting crime
novelists writing today.

Jack Taylor, traumatised, bitter and hurting from his last case, has
resolved to give up the finding business. However, he owes the local hard
man a debt of honour and it appears easy enough: find "the Angel of the
Magdalen" – a woman who helped the unfortunates incarcerated in the
infamous laundry.

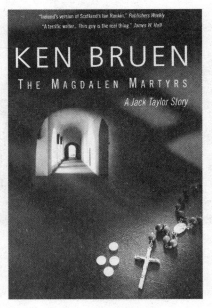

"Outstanding. . . . Ireland's version of Scotland's Ian Rankin."
Publishers Weekly

"Irish writer Ken Bruen is the finest purveyor of intelligent Brit-noir."
The Big Issue

"Why the hell haven't I heard of Ken Bruen before? He's a terrific writer
and *The Guards* is one of the most mesmerizing works of crime fiction
I've ever read. . . This guy is the real thing." James W. Hall

ISBN 0 86322 302 8; Paperback